SEPARATE FROM THE WORLD

AN OHIO AMISH MYSTERY

P. L. Gaus

Ohio University Press
Athens

Ohio University Press, Athens, Ohio 45701
www.ohioswallow.com
© 2008 by P. L. Gaus

To obtain permission to quote, reprint, or otherwise reproduce or
distribute material from Ohio University Press publications, please
contact our rights and permissions department at (740) 593-1154
or (740) 593-4536 (fax).

Printed in the United States of America
Ohio University Press books are printed on acid-free paper ⊗™

15 14 13 12 11 10 09 08   5 4 3 2 1

Library of Congress Cataloging-in-Publication Data

Gaus, Paul L.
  Separate from the world : an Ohio Amish mystery / P.L. Gaus.
    p. cm.
  ISBN 978-0-8214-1814-7 (acid-free paper) — ISBN 978-0-8214-1815-4 (pbk. :
acid-free paper)
   1. Branden, Michael (Fictitious character)—Fiction. 2. College teachers—Fiction.
3. Amish Country (Ohio)—Fiction. 4. Amish—Fiction. I. Title.
  PS3557.A9517S47 2008
  813'.54—dc22
                            2008013987

Dedicated to the memory of my friend Gary Gale.
If height were governed by kindness and decency,
he would have towered over us all.

Preface

THE CHARACTERS in this story are fictional, and none is meant to be a representation in kind, part, or whole of any person, living or dead. The places are real, but they have been used fictitiously. Millersburg College in The Ohio Amish Mysteries is fictional, though several people have assured me that they know right where it is.

Calmoutier (pronounced locally as "Kal-Mooch") is as much a concept in the Amish mind as it is a place. It can be found on some maps, but it is not a city, a town, a burg, a hamlet, or even a crossroads. It is the indefinable area surrounding the old St. Genevieve Church erected by French Catholics in 1836. It lies on the north side of Holmes County Road 229, just east of the Mt. Hope Road and west of where it changes to Nisley Road, in Wayne County. I have been unable to find anyone who can explain the strange pronunciation of Calmoutier.

I have used this area for the story because it is so quintessentially Amish. The story takes place on two Amish farms on a stretch of straight, level road. Purists will note, however, that there is no stretch of 229 that is either straight or level.

Wherefore come out from among them, and be ye separate, saith the Lord.

2 Corinthians 6:17

SEPARATE FROM THE WORLD

1

Wednesday, April 18
5:15 A.M.

LITTLE ALBERT ERB, four years old and dressed Amish to match all the men of his congregation, tackled the steps to the back porch of his house one at a time in the dark, with his most serious frown in place. In his nostrils there lingered the confusion of an unfamiliar odor. Was that how the English smelled, he wondered? Never mind. There were more urgent things to worry about.

Albert stopped to catch his breath on the porch landing, pushed through the heavy back door, and pulled off his blue denim waistcoat in the mudroom. He hung his coat and round-brimmed black hat hastily beside the door, on one of the low hooks for children, and marched into the busy kitchen, thinking he needed to ask again about Mattie.

Why wasn't he allowed to play with her anymore? Something had changed. He wasn't sure what it was, exactly, but he wasn't supposed to see her anymore, and he didn't like that at all. And did they know about the woods—how he went there every day to play with her? Yes—remember to ask about Mattie, he thought.

How could it be wrong to play? Was it the secret they kept that made it wrong? Is that why his father spoke so? Why he felt so ashamed? Albert's thoughts wandered to the woods where they met to play. Mattie always brought one of her puppies. They had fun. He stood in the kitchen, surrounded by family, and puzzled it through in his mind. Why did he have to be secret about playing with her? He knew he did, but why?

Then Albert remembered his uncle Benny, and his puzzlement about Mattie retreated from his thoughts. Uncle Benny was the more important problem right then. Yes—Uncle Benny. Talk to *die Memme* about Benny.

At his mother's side, Albert gave a soft tug on her dress and looked up with innocent brown eyes, searching for her acknowledgment. When she turned to look down at him, he waited for her to speak, as any youngster should.

"Yes, Albert?" she said. "You can see I am busy with breakfast."

Albert nodded gravely, swallowed his consternation, and said, "*Benny vill net schwertze.*"—Benny won't talk.

His mother said, "We're all busy with chores, Albert. Go wash your hands, now, and mind the stove."

Albert kept his gaze on her for a spell, and then shrugged and moved off to the low sink, skirting the wood stove. He was both perplexed about Benny and unhappy with his mother. She didn't have to remind him like that. He'd been burned once, when he was a baby, but he wasn't a baby anymore. He knew about baking biscuits for breakfast. So *die Memme* really didn't have to warn him about hot stoves. He should tell her that, he thought, but when he turned back to show her his pout face, he lost his grasp on his reasons for complaining.

At the sink, he put all of his little weight into pulling down and pushing up on the black iron pump handle, and he rinsed his hands in the cold well water. There, he thought, drying his hands on his pants. Good enough to pass *die Memme*'s inspection.

Albert turned from the sink and went over to his Aunt Lydia at the long kitchen table. He popped up onto the chair beside her and watched her spoon butter into a bowl of fried potatoes.

When she glanced at him, he said, "*Benny kan net laufe.*"—Benny can't walk.

Lydia chided, "You know his legs are stiff, Albert," and got up to pour whole milk from a pail into the dozen glasses set out the night before.

Albert watched her work with the pail, thought about his problem, and decided to tell one of his older brothers. He found Daniel coming into the mudroom with another pail of milk, and he told him, *"Benny kan net tseine."*—Benny can't see.

Daniel nodded, swung past him with the pail, and didn't reply.

So, Albert took his coat and hat off the wall hook and went back outside. He saw a lantern glowing orange in the barn and decided to try to explain his alarm to the *Big Daddy*. Standing outside the milking stall, Albert called out, *"Benny is net u mova, Vater. Her liechusht stille."*—Benny is not moving, Father. He lies still.

For his troubles, all Albert got was, "Albert, tell your sisters to get out here. This milk's going to curdle in the pails."

So, young Albert Erb shrugged his little shoulders, crossed the gravel driveway, and took the sidewalk over to the family's grocery store. Going in at the back, he felt his way down a dark aisle between tall shelves, bent over beside his uncle Benny, and shook his shoulders. Then he pushed on Benny's chest, and nothing happened. Albert sighed, got up on his feet, left the store, and walked back to the big house as the sun streaked a faint line of rose over the horizon. There had been that English aroma again, he realized. He wondered what that meant.

When he took his place at the breakfast table, Albert said to his sister Ella, older than he by two years, *"Benny vil net schwetze."*—Benny won't talk.

Ella laughed and parroted, *"Benny vil net schwetze. Benny vil net schwetze."*

With an indignant scowl, Albert stood on his chair and stomped his boots on the wooden seat. When his mother turned to reprimand him, he flapped his arms up and down at his sides and shouted, *"Benny kan net hicha!"*—Benny can't hear!—determined to make his point.

Before his mother could scold him, Albert's father came into the kitchen with a basket of brown eggs and asked, "Has anyone seen Benny this morning?"

Thus Albert concluded that no one had heard him. Or worse, that no one believed him. He knew he wasn't allowed to be a chatterbox. Didn't Uncle Enos call Benny a chatterbox all the time?

Really, Albert wasn't supposed to talk to grown-ups at all, unless one spoke to him first. Children were meant to be seen, not heard. How many times had they told him that! So this might get him in trouble with the whole family. Maybe I'll take a ribbing from the other kids for this, Albert worried. Maybe I'll have to work all day like the grown-ups. Even though I am only four years old. It might be the last thing I'm allowed to say the whole rest of the day. But it didn't matter. Even in the dark, Albert could tell that there was something dreadfully wrong with his Uncle Benny.

Standing on his chair, with his fists planted on his hip bones, using all the resolve he could muster, little Albert Erb announced, in his very loudest, sternest voice: *"Benny ist im schloffa in die stahe! Al set net das Oatmeal um zie Kopf hawe."*—Benny's sleeping in the store! He's not supposed to have oatmeal on his head like that.

2

Friday, May 11
8:45 A.M.

PROFESSOR MICHAEL BRANDEN sat at his battered walnut
desk, facing a stack of ungraded blue-book final exam essays, in
his office on the second floor of the history building. His mind
wandered as he stared at the essays his students had written the
night before. His thoughts this morning were not focused on grading, and his concentration hadn't improved in the two hours since
he had walked over to campus. For the first time in his life, he wondered if he could face another year as a professor at Millersburg
College.

Branden's academic career was well into its third decade, and
the years he had spent in the classroom were starting to weigh on
him. Perhaps he should have taken that university post, after all.
Or maybe he should have followed his father into the insurance
business. He might have fared better. But now his beard was shot
through with gray, and he was weary of grading like never before.
He wondered whether the college would still pay him if he just let
the grades slide a week or so.

The seniors' exams were finished—they weren't the problem.
Earlier, he had transmitted grades for graduating seniors to the
registrar. Branden was stalled on the final exams written by the
other students, in the lower classes, who didn't really need their
grades for several months. They could wait all summer, if need be.
They would all be back in the fall.

Branden pushed back from his desk, turned his chair to face the windows behind it, and gazed across the main academic quadrangle of the college. Commencement would be held Monday, in three days, in the oak grove beneath his office windows, but why should he bother again? Would it be any different this year? Maybe he wouldn't attend. It wasn't that he begrudged the students their moment on the stage. Rather, it was that the ceremony was so numbingly predictable.

The president would make interminable announcements and proclamations. The speaker would drone on about youthful opportunity, duty, and promise. The chaplain would rehearse a prayer more erudite than honest, and the students would realize afterward, in stunned dismay, that their college years were over. Branden could remember thinking like this in recent years; he really did not like commencements anymore. Maybe that was why the morning had gone so badly for him. Another class would soon disappear. Already, the high school seniors were forming the new class of freshmen, and soon enough they would disappear, too.

Lawrence Mallory knocked abruptly and pushed through Branden's office door, saying, "I'm making coffee, Mike."

Branden shook himself loose from his stupor, turned his chair, flipped his grading pen onto the stack of essays on his desk, and said to his assistant, "Make it strong, Lawrence. It's got to carry me through forty-five more blue books by suppertime."

Mallory eyed the blue books and said, "You haven't finished, Mike?"

"Seniors, yes," Branden replied. "I got them done this morning. But I haven't even started on the others."

Mallory stood in front of Branden's desk, waiting for an explanation.

Branden got slowly to his feet and said, "I don't have it in me, Lawrence."

The professor was of average height and moderate build, though not as slender as he once had been. His salt-and-pepper beard was trimmed to a neat and orderly shortness, and his brown hair was parted, but characteristically ruffled. Today, his eyes carried a weariness that Lawrence could see.

"Once you get started," Lawrence offered, "it'll go fast enough —the same as usual, Mike."

Branden hesitated a moment before meeting his assistant's gaze. "I've been thinking about retirement, Lawrence."

"I don't believe you!"

The thump of heavy boots approached the professor's door. Branden nodded at Mallory and called out, "Come in." When Mallory stepped aside, Branden saw an extremely short man in a hand-made blue denim suit of the Old Order Amish.

The dwarf's graying chin whiskers were long and unruly, lying on his chest. On his head was a black felt winter hat with a perfectly round, three-inch brim and domed crown. His white peasant blouse was tied loosely at the neck. Over it he wore a black vest fastened with hooks and eyes. His work boots were muddy, and his clothes, though not too worn, carried the look of constant labor. Round silver spectacles sat on the end of his nose, and the tops of his white ears poked out through his hat-matted hair. His stunted fingers, creased and calloused, were accented under the nails with the rich black loam of a peasant farm.

Branden stepped around his desk, bent at the waist to offer his hand, and took the little man's puffy palm and stiff fingers into his. The dwarf seemed embarrassed to shake hands, but he shook nevertheless, and asked, in a high, reedy voice, "Are you that professor friend of Cal Troyer's?"

Branden offered the Amish man a chair in front of his desk, and said, "I am Professor Michael Branden. Cal Troyer is my best friend. And this is Lawrence Mallory, my assistant."

Mallory eased past the little person, saying, "I'll check on that coffee," and disappeared into the outer office.

The Amish man nodded gravely to Branden's answer and hopped up onto the front edge of the seat. With his legs swinging free, he asked, "What about Sheriff Robertson?"

Branden laughed, the first relaxed and unguarded thing he'd done that morning, and said, "The sheriff is my best friend, too."

The little man gave a shrug that said, "That seems reasonable, I guess," and followed that with, "I know Caleb Troyer. Can't say as much for the sheriff." Smiling, he added, "It's a happy man who has two best friends."

Branden pulled a wooden office chair over, sat down beside his visitor, and said, "I expect you're not here to question me about my friendships."

"Just wanted to be sure I had the right professor," the Amish dwarf replied.

Branden held his peace, and watched the man turn the brim of his black felt hat through his hardened fingers. The professor knew not to push. This might take some time; it might require the *Amish* kind of time. This fellow would surely need some encouragement before he warmed to his purpose. Branden happily mused that he would have to wait the Amish man out. In truth, he was grateful for the distraction of a slow, deliberate conversation—an oblique Amish-English give and take, until the man was certain that Branden could be trusted. The dwarf would take it slowly, and Branden's morning would not spin along on rapid English time. There was good reason now to ignore those remaining blue books on the desk behind him. At least for a spell.

But Professor Branden was wrong. Direct as an Englisher, and blunt as a cold stone, the little man fixed his gray eyes on the professor and said, "I think my brother was murdered."

3

Friday, May 11
9:00 A.M.

WHEN LAWRENCE brought in two mugs of coffee, Branden was studying the Amish man's eyes for the turmoil and intensity behind the dwarf's surprisingly frank words. But that very English frankness had quickly been replaced by Amish diffidence—the plain people's peaceful resignation to life, which accepts tragedy and fortune as flip sides of the same coin. It is a particularly Amish brand of fatalism, bordering on Zen, and Branden knew it well.

In his Amish self, this man would consider that life and death signified nothing more remarkable than the chance flip to heads or tails. Flip the coin one way, and there was life; flip the other way, and there stood death. We live; we die. It is in God's hands. To understand this is to practice humility—*Demut*—the most beautiful virtue—*de schönste Tegund*.

But Branden had also seen a flash of English hunger when the man had spoken. It was a cold, hollow hunger for English justice, and it would be a sin of contemplation if shown openly to his Amish brothers and sisters. The little man had come in search of the kind of justice that the English world could give him. That Branden, Troyer, and Robertson could give him. And this was a very non-Amish thing for him to have done.

Cocking a hip off his chair, the dwarf fished in his side pocket for a wadded cotton handkerchief. He took off his spectacles, cleaned the glass, and stuffed the handkerchief back into his pocket.

Palms raised, he shrugged his shoulders and said, "No one knows I am here."

Branden accepted a mug of coffee from Lawrence and asked the Amish man, "Do you like coffee?"

The man smiled, said, "Yes, it puts a bounce in my step," and accepted the other mug from Lawrence. Finding the mug too hot, he handed it right back to a startled Lawrence and again fished his handkerchief out of his pants pocket. Then he reached out for the mug, taking the handle in the stubby fingers of his right hand and cradling the bottom of the mug on the wadded handkerchief in his left palm. As Lawrence was leaving, he turned in his chair and said, "Thanks for the coffee."

Mallory stopped in the doorway to say, "Sure. There's more, if you like it."

The professor set his mug on the front corner of his desk, and said, "You have the advantage of me, sir. You know my name, but I don't know yours."

The little man laughed, hoisted his mug to his lips, sipped, and said, "Enos Erb. Of the Samuel Erbs. Brother to Israel and Benjamin. I've got the farm across the road from Israel's, out at Calmoutier. He's farming the homestead lands. It's Benjamin, 'Benny,' who's dead."

"Benny was Samuel's son? Samuel is your father, too?"

"Yep. Our father is Samuel, and our mother is Annie. Benny lived in an apartment next to the Grossvater Haus we built for our parents when Israel took over the big farm. Benny never married, so he stayed on with Israel. Israel and I support them all. Plus Lydia Weaver, who is Hannah's sister."

"And Hannah is?"

"Israel's wife. She's a Weaver. Daughter of David and Vesta Weaver. David has been dead for nearly fifteen years. Hannah's mother, Vesta, lives with the Levi Klines down the road—with Hannah's sister, Mary, who married Levi Kline."

"And you'll have other siblings," Branden offered, and took up his coffee again.

There was an outcry from someplace on campus, perhaps at the far edge of the oak grove, Branden thought. He pictured the seniors starting their revelries, finished at last with exams and launching the weekend celebrations, prior to Monday's commencement. His memories fell across the years long gone, and he shook his head. The weekend parties had deteriorated in twenty years from pleasant social events that the faculty might reasonably attend, to unrestrained, nearly continuous intoxicated spectacles. This year it seemed that Friday morning would mark the start of it all. Another good reason to retire, Branden thought.

The Amish visitor watched the thoughts drift across the professor's face, waited patiently for them to pass, and spoke when Branden looked back to him.

"You asked about our family, Professor," the little man said. "Israel and I are two of twelve. Hannah and Mary are two of fifteen. Most have moved away. We have sisters who married men up in Middlefield. And brothers who've moved to Kentucky and Ontario. We're all kind of spread out now, because land is so tight around here. So, mostly, it's me and Israel who are the Erbs of Calmoutier. And Lydia, Mary, and Hannah, who used to be Weavers. I guess Lydia still is a Weaver, because she never married."

"I think I should be taking notes, Enos," Branden said dryly.

Enos laughed. "I'll write it out for you."

"That'll help."

Through the open windows, Branden and his visitor could hear the distant chanting of a protest rally against the war in Iraq. A bullhorn prompted with a slogan, and the crowd responded, parroting the words: "Bush lied and people died!" repeated several times. Then the prompt, "U.S.—Never best!" and the crowd's response with the same phrase time and again. When the shouts died off, a speech could be heard coming from a P.A. sound system, but

Branden and Erb could not make out the words. No doubt, Branden mused, it was psychology professor Aidan Newhouse leading another of his antiwar rallies on campus. Still reliving the sixties.

Enos observed, "It's pretty wild outside, and I'm not talking about that protest group. No. I saw two students, just now. That boy was sure getting some action off his girl, and you'd better believe it."

Branden smiled. "It's the seniors. They'll graduate on Monday."

Enos shrugged. "They were out in the parking lot where I left my buggy. He had her pinned against his car—kissing out in the open."

"They're just college kids, Enos," Branden offered, wondering how to explain the excesses of college life to a man who had devoted himself to plain living.

Looking right at Branden, Enos asked bluntly, "Do you get some action off those college girls, too, Professor? I've heard professors can be like that."

Branden's back straightened, and heat flashed into his cheeks. In his present mood, he was powerless to hide his indignant anger. He let it display itself briefly and then quenched it.

Of all the Amish people he knew, few were capable of guile. There was, perhaps, the occasional inconsiderate bluntness in conversation, or an untoward curiosity about the suspect English lifestyles, but certainly no guile. With a mix of alarm and amusement, he eyed the little man and answered simply, "No, Mr. Erb. I am happily married."

Enos nodded with a degree of satisfaction, drained the last of his coffee, and asked, "Your man said there was more?" lifting his empty mug.

Branden got out of his chair smiling broadly at the man's directness, went out to Mallory's front office, brought the carafe back, and poured more of the morning's brew into Enos Erb's mug.

The siren of an ambulance started up in the distance, and it mixed soon with the bleat of a sheriff's cruiser. The sirens came nearer, mounted the college heights, and flashed by the history building to draw up on the other side of the oak grove, in front of the old stone chapel.

Branden stepped to his windows and saw a crowd of students and faculty standing in a ragged circle on the far side of the grove, in front of the chapel. When the paramedics ran up to the group, the crowd parted to let them through, and the professor saw a young woman, college age, in jeans and a white blouse, face down on the chapel's stone walkway, blood pooling beside her head. The paramedics rolled her onto her back, and her head came to rest facing the professor's office. In the instant that he recognized her, numbing shock and sorrow coursed through Branden's veins, and the professor whispered, "Cathy." He had just seen her final exam in his stack of ungraded blue books.

One of the girls standing beside the body started gesturing dramatically toward the tall bell tower of the chapel, and the people on the ground craned their necks to look up in unison.

Branden followed their gaze, but was unable to see because of the tall trees. Dazed and fighting denial, he moved to his left-most window. Between the top branches of a tree, he caught sight of a senior he recognized, standing bare-chested on the bell tower's parapet. The boy seemed frozen to the stone, staring down at the dead girl, his face a blank mask of horror, his hair disheveled and sprouting out as if charged from electroshock.

Branden's mind flooded with images of the two students, one now dead and one now perched on the edge of disaster. He saw them as he remembered them, in the classroom, holding hands on the sidewalk, carrying trays together through the dining room. They'd rarely been separated since they had started dating. Cathy and Eddie. They were his students.

Branden tried to get his mind to settle on the dreadful present, but he couldn't catch up to the pace of his thoughts. He recognized this mental state. He taught about it in his Civil War classes—the fog of battle, brought on by horror and panic. The mind rendered useless by shock. An eerie, otherworldly kind of detachment from one's normal capabilities. Soldiers frozen in place by the paralyzing spectacle that was assaulting their eyes. And he realized he'd be lucky in this fog simply to get his feet to move.

Branden's eyes fell back to the crumpled body of his student, and he sensed that Enos Erb was standing beside him, on his tiptoes, looking down over the windowsill at the death scene.

When he realized what he was looking at, Erb blurted out, "Oh, my!" and ran out of the professor's office. Mallory took his place at the windows.

Branden pulled his gaze back to the bell tower and saw Cathy Billett's boyfriend standing with his arms spread wide, as if preparing to launch himself into flight. There was a shout from the crowd below, and the boy's balance wobbled on the rail. Branden sucked air through his teeth and felt the muscles and tendons in his legs tighten involuntarily to the snapping point. Eddie pitched forward, arms flying, and then righted his balance. He looked blankly out over the treetops like a stage actor peering into floodlights, and seemed to resign himself to death. His face went slack, his eyes closed, and he put one foot out over the edge just as a sheriff's deputy darted up behind him and clamped his fist onto Eddie's belt, hauling him forcefully back from the edge.

Eddie screamed and spun around to swing at the man. The officer stepped underneath a wild, roundhouse punch. He pinned Eddie's arm behind his back and hit him in the kidney to drop him to the roof, putting the two of them below the level of the parapet and out of sight to Branden and Mallory. After a moment, the deputy stood up, drew the flat of his palms over cropped black hair, and blew out a tense breath. Then he turned, stepped over to the edge, and looked down to wave at Sheriff Bruce Robertson below.

In his frozen panic, Branden had not noticed Robertson among the crowd on the ground. When he looked back up to the parapet, Branden realized he also had not recognized Sergeant Ricky Niell.

He should be doing something, Branden realized. He should be down there with Cathy. He should move. His eyes played mechanically from ground to parapet and back again, and he forced himself to breathe. He sensed that his legs were waiting for his mind to clear. He tried flexing his fingers and found them clenched into fists. He purposefully trained his eyes on the bell tower and was grateful for this one remnant of command that was still his. The scene there seemed unnaturally calm.

Sergeant Niell brushed off his uniform shirt, tucked the tails under his duty belt, and straightened a gold pen in his shirt pocket. He motioned down for more men to come up to the roof, and then turned, pulled the handcuffed senior to his feet, and started walking him over to the interior stone steps that would take them back through the belfry and down to the crowd milling around the dead girl's body.

4

Friday, May 11
9:15 A.M.

WHEN THE PROFESSOR realized that the cry he had heard while talking with Enos Erb had been his student falling to her death, he was finally able to force his feet to move. He stepped haltingly out of his office suite, started running in the hall, took the steps two at a time, and bolted out into the oak grove beneath his office windows. He ran across the expanse of lawn under the oaks and arrived at the ambulance just as paramedics were pulling their orange-padded gurney out of the back.

Sheriff Robertson waved impatiently for the paramedics to move forward. He spotted the professor and stepped up to him, barking, "What gives, Mike? You've never had a suicide up here! Not in forty years!"

"I know the girl!" Branden cried.

Robertson pulled the professor aside and asked for a name.

"Cathy Billett. She's a junior," Branden said, pulling at his hair, eyes wide with alarm. "That fellow over there in handcuffs is Eddie Hunt-Myers. He's a senior. Bruce, I can't believe this! They both took my final exam last night."

"Would she have taken the 'express' off a bell tower over a stupid exam?" Robertson asked, indelicately. "Why would she do this, Mike?"

"No! She was a good student. Eddie too." Taking a step forward, Branden complained, "Come on. Does he have to be in cuffs, like that?"

Robertson pulled him back. "He took a swing at Ricky Niell, Mike."

"I saw that, Bruce. It's more like he was going to jump, and Ricky surprised him from behind. He was just startled. I think you can take those cuffs off him now."

Robertson frowned as he studied the professor's expression. "He one of your little rich boys, Mike?"

"Knock it off!" Branden snapped. He paced an anxious circle in front of Robertson, who was still blocking him from the body. Some of the heat drained out of the professor when he realized he would not get past the large sheriff.

Sheriff Bruce Robertson had grown up a simple, small-town Buckeye, a friend from kindergarten of both Branden and Cal Troyer. Heavyset since childhood, in late middle age he was becoming "excessive." His wife, Coroner Missy Taggert, had convinced him to stop smoking and lose weight when they married, but although he had succeeded at the first of her requests, he had failed at the second. His uniform fit too snugly, and his imposing bulk served as an unfortunate ally of his blunt and sometimes immoderate personality. He was the size of a bull and, when he was off his medicines, as impulsive as an overindulged teenager.

While Branden paced, there was an outburst from the crowd near the dead girl's body. When Branden and Robertson looked over, they saw Ricky Niell pulling Eddie Hunt-Myers, still in handcuffs, away from an angry girl, who was slapping at Niell's back and shoulders, as she hurled invectives. The Iraq War protesters had arrived from the far side of campus, led by Professor Aidan Newhouse, and some of them took up the girl's side, shouting at Niell about police misconduct. Soon the crowd's protests swelled to resemble the ruckus of a small mob.

A female deputy Branden did not recognize took hold of the angry girl's shoulders and managed to wrap her arms around her and pull her back from Niell. Some members of the crowd made a surge in Niell's direction, spurred on by the girl's fury, as two more deputies planted themselves between the protesters and Ricky Niell.

There was a shout, "Let him go!" and a snarl from another voice, "Take your hands off me!" Someone barked, "No cops!" and several voices repeated the cry.

Professor Newhouse spoke a few calming words to try to settle his students down as he moved among them, asking for more restraint. But Newhouse's students had taken his course about "The Sixties" to heart. The chant rang out: "NO COPS! NOT HERE! NOT AGAIN!" Newhouse persisted, however, and with great effort he was able to prevail. The protesters fell momentarily quiet. As they stood in place, eyeing Niell with evident scorn, one of the sheriff's deputies took up a position too close to the protesters, and scuffling broke out again.

Seeing the anger rising, Niell hustled his bare-chested prisoner over to his cruiser and pulled the back door open, stuffing the boy inside. The shouts from the crowd peaked when Niell closed the door of the cruiser, with the senior Eddie Hunt-Myers struggling awkwardly in the back, hands pinned behind him, a dazed confusion frozen on his face.

Robertson waded into the crowd like a bulldozer, pushing people back from the paramedics, who were struggling to load the dead girl's body onto their gurney. College security officers arrived on foot and helped move the most vocal and irate critics back several steps. And the mob fell suddenly silent when tall, lanky Ben Capper, the chief of security for the college, barked through a megaphone, "Stand back! Right now! I'm not going to tell you again."

Capper had a fierce glare in his eyes, and his bony fingers were locked onto the grip of his megaphone as if he were strangling a rattlesnake. The muscles in his face clenched and bunched over strong cheekbones and a cleft chin. His black hair, cut to a military style, was standing up on end, as if he'd just waxed it into place. He was a military man in a boring job, looking for purpose, and his eyes promised trouble for anyone who would defy him.

The crowd of students and professors responded to the intensity of his command, seeming to back-pedal a half-dozen steps while still holding together as a loose mob. Their postures promised that they were ready to surge again.

Niell walked over from his cruiser, took the megaphone from Capper, and announced calmly but sternly, "This is your friend here on the gurney. Show some respect."

Newhouse stepped forward and said, "Your work is done, here, Sheriff. You need to leave. We want no cops on our campus."

One fellow in the crowd shouted, "No cops!" and others took up his lead, chanting, "NO COPS! NO COPS!" as if it were an antiwar rally over Vietnam, or Iraq.

Professor Newhouse raised his hands for everyone to see and silenced the crowd. Again he said to Robertson, "You need to leave, Sheriff."

Robertson started to address the man, but Branden came up behind him and said, "You need to move your people off campus with the ambulance, Sheriff, and let this guy burn himself out on adrenalin. He'll whip up this crowd, if you let him bait you like this. He hates police. He's gonna try to make this a civil rights issue, and you don't want that."

Disliking it intensely, Robertson nevertheless took Branden's advice. He gave Niell a hand signal, took hold of the side rail on the gurney, and started the paramedics back toward the ambulance with the dead girl's body. Once she was loaded, the deputies got into their cruisers and followed Niell out of the oak grove and down off the college heights into town.

With the sheriff's people gone, the crowd lost heat quickly and began to thin out. Newhouse corralled the remnant, saying quietly, "I've seen all this before. Cops have no business taking one of us away in handcuffs!"

A student at his side shouted out again, "No cops! No cops!" but Newhouse laid a strong hand on his shoulder and caused him to stop, saying, "We'll be back at the courthouse this afternoon for our Iraq protests. That's the time to deal with our sheriff. In the meantime, study the tactics of the police in arresting the Chicago

Seven. Study up on this. I want you to appreciate what it is you saw here."

Aidan Newhouse was one of the most senior professors on campus. His gray hair was tied back severely into a thin ponytail, and his skin was pasty white and mottled with old acne scars. He had an angular jawline that accented his ire when he struck a stubborn or disgruntled pose. Most of the time he was angry about one thing or disappointed about another, and he harbored an animosity toward police that he was quick to explain to anyone who would listen. He'd spent several nights in a small-town southern jail in his college years, arrested during protests in the sixties.

A core of a dozen people, students mostly but some faculty too, formed a circle around their leader and kept vigil while he lectured about cops, Vietnam, and "the movement." This was grand theater to him—the true classroom. It was a teachable moment, served up to him more perfectly than he himself could have devised. It was a true pity about the girl, he thought, but he would no more waste this moment than he would surrender his professorship. He'd taught about the sixties for many long years, and as he spoke, he felt the intense and dynamic emotions of a true believer, set free at last to answer the call of his generation.

*　*　*

Chief of Security Ben Capper watched the crowd disperse until there remained only Professor Aidan Newhouse and six students. As Newhouse droned on about the sixties, Capper listened at a distance and knew that here was real trouble.

"Aidan Newhouse" was a file as thick as a dictionary in Ben Capper's security office, and Capper knew that Newhouse would do just about anything to relive the glories of his youth. He was a shrill anti-Iraq war protester, and the clear leader of the groups who had taken to marching down at the courthouse square. Capper knew them all too well.

He knew the protest songs they played over their loudspeakers —Jimi Hendrix, doing Bob Dylan's "All Along the Watchtower." That Neil Young group doing "Four Dead in Oh Hi Oh." The Doors. Jefferson Airplane. Janis Joplin. He knew the songs, and he knew the chants. He'd seen all their signs and placards before, when he came home from Vietnam. Ben Capper had been here before. These were the people who had spit on him when he got off the plane from Saigon. He knew what these people could do.

But Ben Capper knew Aidan Newhouse best of all. He was the worst—a Marxist instigator. An America hater. A flag burner. And many times now, Capper had promised himself that if that hippie professor ever burned an American flag on the campus grounds, he'd club the insufferable toad into paste.

The trouble was, Newhouse was the worst sort of person to provoke, and if he ever found out that Capper had been keeping a file on him, he'd organize, that very day, a hundred grungy students to protest in front of President Laughton's residence, demanding the chief of security's resignation. Newhouse was that detestable type of bully who, if given even half a chance, would end Ben Capper's career over a trifle.

* * *

Mike Branden stood alone in the oak grove, several dozen yards away from Professor Newhouse, and again found himself unable to move. He was vaguely aware of the problem, but could not respond to it. Or perhaps he was unwilling to respond. Unwilling to move. He did not know for sure. He was stunned like a soldier in the fog.

He did not have to hear Newhouse's words to understand what the psychology professor was saying. The two of them had debated the issues of the sixties enough to be able to recite one another's very thoughts. Newhouse was born to be a dissenter. He was bred to be an activist. He had been annealed to an academician's life by the events of his youth, and he truly and everlastingly believed the things he taught. Branden found himself smiling weakly and shaking his head as he realized how perfect this moment was for Newhouse the teacher—an authority despiser since the days of teargas and police dogs on the nation's campuses.

But Cathy Billett was dead, Branden's student Eddie Hunt-Myers was down at the jail, maybe still in handcuffs, and the professor couldn't get his mind to work for the second time that day. His contemplation of retirement and his weariness with his profession had now been washed through with a cleansing rinse of shock and sorrow, making all of his dissatisfactions seem trivial. Cathy Billett had died within view of his office windows. Which of his disaffections mattered now?

Though his heart was wet with tears, and his feet were cased in lead, he managed somehow to turn and start moving. He had only a distant notion that he should go somewhere, and after a few steps, he found he was headed home. He did not care where he was going, really. He merely followed his instincts to move forward in his sorrow, still in the fog of shock.

In slow, irregular steps, he moved through the oak grove to the curb. His eyes were focused inward, but when he turned toward the parking lot behind the history building, he saw the dwarf Enos Erb guiding a buggy out of the lot. Branden's vision seemed focused only on Erb and his buggy. His sight was tunneled, and the rest of the world around him was a blur.

Erb drove a black buggy of regular size, hitched to a brown Standard Bred horse. He sat on the seat with his legs out straight, balanced like a bowling ball on a porch swing. Erb turned his horse in Branden's direction, came up to him slowly, and stopped his buggy at the curb beside him. There was both sorrow and alarm in his eyes.

Erb whispered, "Is that poor girl really dead?"

Branden nodded.

Erb studied his hands on the reins for several beats and then asked, "If sex is free, Professor, then what is left to cherish in marriage?"

Branden tipped his head, but provided no answer.

A long pause lay between the two men, and then Erb said, "Professor, that girl was young."

Branden nodded. He had no words to offer.

Erb asked, "Do they really live together? Do they know each other's bodies like the bumps on their own heads?"

"I suppose," Branden said, feeling weariness at the core.

"We hear about these things," Erb remarked, aware of the professor's sorrow. He shook his head and added, "I've never seen a dead girl like that before. You know, a suicide."

Because Branden could think of nothing better to say, he responded simply, "I'm sorry you saw that, Mr. Erb," and added in a whisper, "She was my student."

Gently, Erb said, "I'm sorry for you, Professor. I am truly so very sorry. I don't know what to say. Our children die, too, you see. We lose them to diseases and highway crashes with cars. There are sometimes accidents on the farm. Yes, we know death well, even the death of children. But not like that. Not suicide, Professor. I can't tell you that I know anything about suicide."

Branden said nothing. His eyes were focused on the pavement, and he could not think what reply he might make to this simplest of men. He could not think how any reply could be adequate. How anyone could understand what had happened. Really, he couldn't think at all. He was still in the fog.

5

Friday, May 11
10:00 A.M.

IT WAS TWO short blocks to the Brandens' brick house on a cul-
de-sac near the college, but it took the professor twenty minutes to
walk it. He unlocked the front door with a surreal mechanical
fumbling, stepped inside, and walked down the front hallway to
the kitchen, where he found a note on his wife's stationery. He ran
his eyes over the handwritten letters several times before the words
came into focus:

> You'll be done soon, Sweetheart.
> Try not to be morose.
> I know you don't like commencements anymore,
> but Monday will come and go as quickly as ever.
>
> Cal has news.
> I'm down at his church.
>
> > Love,
> > Caroline

Branden let Caroline's note slip back onto the table, and he took
a cleansing breath. His eyes found the wooden bench at the end of
their long backyard, and he remembered the dwarf's words: "I think
my brother was murdered."

At the hall closet, Branden got out of his sandals and padded into the living room. The soft carpet was cool on his feet, and he discovered that he could think clearly about that. About the cool carpet. Just that for now, but it was enough. It was familiar. The soft carpet registered with him reassuringly. He dropped into a swivel rocker and looked around at the familiar room. Here is where he sat to read—in this soft chair. There is the couch where Caroline read each night. The photographs on the wall were scenes he recognized, beach scenes from Michigan and red barns and farm fields from the Holmes County countryside. With the thought, "This is home," his mind cleared partially, and he thought about Eddie Hunt-Myers. He thought about the handcuffs. He remembered his duty to his student, and he rose, walked back to the hall closet, and slipped back into his sandals.

As he walked through the laundry room to the garage, he covered his T-shirt with a yellow windbreaker. He backed his small white truck out onto the street and drove down to the courthouse, thinking of Enos Erb saying—"Then what is left to cherish in marriage?"

*   *   *

The professor parked his truck in the courthouse alley behind the red brick jail and hurried around to the north entrance, past the tall Civil War monument. Inside, to the right, he found Ellie Troyer-Niell behind her wooden counter, seated with her back to him, clicking the mouse on her computer. When he said, "Hi, Ellie," she turned around and said, "I hear you had trouble up at the college."

"One of my students," Branden said softly, hating the sound of his words. "Evidently a suicide."

"I'm sorry, Mike. I didn't know she was your student."

"In my history class," Branden said. "Bruce brought in her boyfriend?"

"Not here, he didn't," Ellie said. "They're all up at the hospital."

Branden nodded and turned to go.

Ellie said, "I'm really sorry about your student, Mike."

"Thanks," Branden said, and turned back to her. "You know anything about the recent murder of a Benjamin Erb? An Amish fellow?"

"Missy ruled that accidental," Ellie said.

"Do you know what happened?"

"The man fell off a ladder, is all I know. Broke his neck in a fall."

"OK, thanks," Branden said, and left, remembering Erb's directness—"I think my brother was murdered."

* * *

On the Wooster Road north of the courthouse, Branden turned right onto the hillside grounds of Joel Pomerene Memorial Hospital. He parked downhill from the rear entrance and walked through sliding glass doors into Melissa Taggert's coroner's suite in the basement.

In the antiseptic hallway outside the office and labs, he found Ricky Niell awash in harsh fluorescent lighting, taking notes on a spiral pad while listening to Eddie Hunt-Myers, who was out of his handcuffs. Hunt-Myers still looked stunned, hair disheveled.

He was a tall, powerfully built Floridian, with a butternut tan and bleached blond hair that suggested he'd been out in the sun on spring break. His eyebrows were blond and bushy, and the blond hairs of his chest were a tangle at the neckline of the green hospital scrubs he wore. His blue eyes roamed restlessly from place to place as he talked, and his hands worked nervously in front of his chest. Coming closer, Branden could see that Eddie's eyelids were red and swollen—he'd obviously been crying, and there was a scattering of wadded tissues on the floor at his feet. When he saw Branden, Eddie croaked out, "Help me, Dr. Branden! I think I'm losing my mind."

Branden came up beside Ricky Niell and asked, "Do you have what you need for now?"

"Think so," Niell said. He looked at Eddie, shook his head, and asked the professor, "You knew the girl, too?"

Eddie folded at the knees and dropped to the floor, crying, "I can't believe this is happening."

Niell and Branden helped the boy up, and Branden sat on a hallway bench with him.

Ricky asked, "You got this, Mike? Can you sit here with him?"

Branden nodded and gave his attention to Eddie.

Ricky said, "Then I'm going to find the sheriff," and moved down the hall.

Eddie started rocking back and forth on the seat and groaning while he wrung his hands in his lap. "He thinks I hurt her, Dr. Branden," he said. "They think I hurt Cathy."

Branden laid his hand on Eddie's shoulder and said, "Take it easy, now, Eddie," but Eddie flinched at the touch, and tears streamed down his cheeks.

Through his own sorrow, Branden said, "We'll get through this, Eddie."

Eddie shouted, "I won't! Not ever!" and jumped to his feet, punching his fists against the sides of his head as if he wanted to crush his skull, to force the images of Cathy Billett from his mind.

Branden got up and pulled Eddie's fists to his sides, saying, "Sit down, Eddie. Tell me what happened." He had to wrap Eddie's fingers in his hands to keep him from tearing at his hair.

Eddie let the professor guide him back to the bench. With a look of utter misery, Eddie whispered, "I did this, Professor. They're right. I killed Cathy. I might as well have thrown her off the tower myself."

Branden said, "Tell me what happened, Eddie," and let go of the boy's hands.

Eddie wrapped his arms across his stomach and started rocking again where he sat. He looked over briefly at the professor and then fixed his gaze at the far wall. Still whispering, he said, "I told her I didn't want us to be together anymore. I loved her, but I told her we were through."

"Eddie," Branden started, then stalled.

Eddie shot another glance at the professor and said, "It's my fault. It's my fault, and now she's dead. I still love her, Dr. Branden. I still feel her. But I knew we had to break up, and I told her that this morning. That's when she ran to the edge and jumped."

* * *

Sheriff Robertson stood farther down the hall, leaning his considerable bulk into the doorway to Missy Taggert's office, and from the tone of his voice, Branden surmised that he was not happy right then with his wife.

Leaving Niell in charge of Eddie Hunt-Myers, Branden came up behind the sheriff, who was saying, "Look, Missy, I need to know if this was really a suicide. I think he killed her, but you tell me."

Taggert gave no reply that Branden could hear, and Robertson backed out of the doorway as the door was pushed closed from the other side.

Holmes County Coroner and Medical Examiner Melissa Taggert was a striking woman several years younger than her husband and Branden. Her soft brown hair was usually done up in a bun so she could wear an autopsy cap over it. Though considerably more slender than her husband, Missy was strongly and solidly built, and when she didn't like his intrusions on her work, she just pushed him back through the door, saying, "Bruce, you're gonna have to let me work." Thus Sheriff Robertson found himself in the hallway.

Robertson got himself turned around and spotted Branden. "I'm not real happy about getting run off your college up there, Mike."

Branden nodded. He appreciated the reasons for the sheriff's ire, but he squared up to his friend. "You had to leave, Bruce. Aidan Newhouse was going to provoke you. That's what he does. He craves attention, especially from the law. Since Vietnam, he's been looking for excuses to march again. I know he's made a pest of himself at the courthouse, leading his students against the Iraq war. If you'd stayed there, you would have had a hundred people shouting at 'the pigs' in no time at all."

Robertson acknowledged the point and seemed to deflate in front of the professor. In a calmer tone, he said to Branden, "I've sent Dan Wilsher and Pat Lance back up there in plainclothes. That bell tower needs a look."

Branden nodded approval. He noted with relief that he was starting to think clearly again. "What has Eddie told you?"

Robertson scowled. "Says they made love last night on the tower. Then he broke up with her this morning, and she threw herself off the tower, on account of it."

"You don't believe him?" Branden asked.

"I'll wait to hear from Dan and Pat. If there was a lover's quarrel, the top of that bell tower might have some evidence of it."

"I know these two, Bruce," Branden said. "They're my students. They were in my classes. They were in love. Eddie could no more have hurt Cathy Billett than he could have stopped his own heart."

Saying this, Branden found himself sorting through his thoughts, even as he confronted his sorrow. He realized that Eddie's confession had given him a better reason to move forward than anything else could have. These were his students. He knew them. "Eddie thinks he's responsible, but he did not kill her, Bruce," he added. "He hasn't got the capacity."

Robertson stared back at the professor for a long couple of seconds and said, "Like I said, Mike. Dan and Pat are up there now. I'll wait to hear what they have to say."

Branden smiled. This was high diplomacy for the gruff sheriff. Whatever he told Robertson now would fall on deaf ears. Robertson was walled off and tunnel sighted. The professor decided to change the subject.

"I don't know Pat Lance," Branden said.

"I hired her in November, after Kessler officially retired. Dan Wilsher is chief deputy now."

"What's her background?"

"Pat Lance? She's an investigator/criminalist. Out of the Air National Guard, over in Mansfield. Came back from Iraq last summer."

"And you're using her as a simple deputy? Not as a detective?"

"She can move onto a desk when she's earned a stripe or two."

"She any good?"

Robertson nodded. "She's military, Mike. You know I like that."

"What I meant was, is she too good to use in a cruiser?"

"She can start like everyone else. If she wants better, she knows she has to show me something."

"Did you explain it to her in those terms, Sheriff?"

"Like anyone else, Professor," Robertson said. He glanced down the hall. "Your rich boy, there, looks like a playboy to me, all tanned to bronze like that."

At the end of the hall, Eddie sat down on the bench again, cradling his head in his hands. Ricky Niell started forward with his spiral notepad.

Branden said, "He's not *my boy*, Bruce. He's my student. And it doesn't matter that his parents are wealthy."

Niell advanced with his eyes focused on a page, and said, "He says that he killed her. Not that he did it, but that he's to blame, because he broke up with her."

"He told me the same thing," said Branden. "He feels responsible for her death. He's not only grieving, he's in shock."

Robertson turned to Branden and said, "He's a playboy, Mike."

"He's just a college kid, Bruce," Branden argued. "He's supposed to march in commencement Monday morning and take his diploma home to Florida. He'll work in his family's boatyard. Cathy Billett was from a cattle ranch in Montana. She was going home to her family. Couples like that break up a lot this time of year. They think they'll never be able to make it in a long-distance relationship, and they just give up."

The sheriff's cell phone chirped. He checked his display, took the call, and said, "Yeah, Dan. What have you got? I'm putting you on speaker phone."

Robertson held the phone out, and the three men heard Chief Deputy Wilsher say, "The roof of this bell tower looks like an all-night frat-house party, Sheriff. It's pretty much a mess, but there are girl's shoes and a large man's button-down shirt. A wine bottle, beer cans, and some condoms."

Branden said, "The tower's supposed to be locked, Dan."

"Well, it's not," Wilsher said. "There's an old sleeping bag laid out here, and a shredded wine cork that looks like it was carved out with a knife. There's a little penknife lying here, too."

Ricky said, "That's all consistent with what Hunt-Myers has told me."

"You going to arrest him?" Dan asked over the phone.

Branden groaned and said, "No, Bruce. That'd be wrong."

Robertson thought, shook his head, and said, "Naw. No arrest, Dan. Not for now."

Over the phone, Wilsher said, "Wait," and a moment later, "Maybe you'd better get back up on campus, Bruce. Ben Capper has some hippie professor locked in handcuffs. I'm looking down at them now."

Ricky spoke toward the phone, "College security guards aren't supposed to carry handcuffs."

Wilsher came back, "Well, yeah. But neither is the chief of college security supposed to be holding an ice pack to his eye."

Branden said, "Bruce, if you go back up there, you'll be poking a stick into a hornet's nest."

Robertson said, "Hang on, Dan," and muted his phone. Growling, he said, "Mike, I don't have any choice here."

"You do, Bruce," Branden said. "Just tell Dan and Pat Lance to pack Newhouse and Capper up and bring them both down here."

Robertson unmuted his phone and asked, "Dan, can you just put Ben Capper and that professor in your car and bring them both down to the jail?"

Wilsher said, "Lance already has Capper in the backseat."

Urgently, Branden said, "Dan, listen. Get Newhouse out of those cuffs."

"I'll talk to him," Wilsher said.

"No, Dan, listen," Branden said. "He wants to be in those cuffs. You're gonna make a martyr out of a mouse."

There was a pause, and next Deputy Lance came on the phone. "Sheriff, Pat Lance here. Chief Wilsher is taking the cuffs off, now."

Robertson bit down on his more assertive instincts, and said, "You and Dan bring Capper in alone, Lance."

Then Lance said, "This professor is nuts, Sheriff. Won't let us take the cuff off his other wrist."

Branden muttered, "I've been doing this too long." He flashed the mental image of a dwarf Amish man balanced on the flat seat of a black buggy, asking about college kids and sex, and he groaned. He looked down to Eddie, still on the hallway bench, and asked Niell, "Ricky, can you take Eddie back to campus?"

Niell nodded, "Sure," and Branden started walking down the hall.

* * *

The professor's phone rang, and he answered it in the hallway, feeling spent. Caroline was right. He had been morose. He was feeling the years.

Arne Laughton, president of Millersburg College, asked, "Mike, where are you?"

"Medical examiner's labs, with Bruce Robertson."

"Has he taken Eddie Hunt-Myers into custody?"

"What?"

"Eddie Hunt-Myers. Is he in custody? I got a call from his father."

"Arne, Cathy Billett is dead. You need to be down here."

"Can't come now, Mike. Edwin Hunt-Myers is an alumnus. He just wants to know where his boy is."

Branden moved outside to the parking lot and said, "Arne, I'm only going to tell you this once. Cathy Billett's family deserves your consideration more, right now, than anyone else. You let me take care of Eddie. You need to help the Billetts."

"They're saying it was suicide, Mike. I can't call her parents until I know about that."

Incredulous, Branden demanded, "You haven't called them?"

"It's only been an hour, Mike. Do you think this was a suicide?"

"Yes," Branden said, feeling dirty. "Missy Taggert has her body in the morgue."

Laughton urged, "Ask her, Mike. Find out for me. Then I'll make that call."

"Look, Arne," the professor said, "you're gonna blow this. Think. Cathy is dead because they got into the bell tower last night."

There was silence on the line. Then Laughton said, "I'll be there as soon as I can."

"Come now," Branden said. "You can stand outside the morgue and provide some comfort for Eddie. I'm going to leave."

Laughton held the connection, but did not reply. Feeling the weight of his years, Branden said, "Arne, this is not your finest hour."

6

Friday, May 11
10:45 A.M.

BRUCE ROBERTSON found Branden standing on the hospital's blacktop, next to his white truck. The professor still had his phone out, but it was closed.

"Who was that?" Robertson asked.

"Arne Laughton."

"Is he coming down?"

"Says he is. Look, Bruce, I'm gonna go find Caroline. And I've got to talk to Cal about an Amish fellow. You going to be OK with this for a while?"

The sheriff said, "You know I don't like Laughton."

"Right now, I don't either," Branden said.

"I'm gonna wait to hear what Missy says," Robertson said. "I'm sending your boy home with Ricky, but he's not off the hook. Not with me. I want to know if he pushed her off that tower."

"You're wrong about him, Bruce. As wrong as you can be."

"You let me worry about Eddie Hunt-Myers, Mike. You've got a reserve deputy sheriff's badge, and I want you to use it now. I need you to stay here and handle Arne Laughton for me."

Branden rubbed at tension in the back of his neck and pictured Arne Laughton back on the phone with Eddie's father. The cord that tethered Branden emotionally to the college seemed to him more frayed than ever. "Try not to be morose," he remembered from Caroline's note. He saw Cathy Billett lying on the ground and Eddie swaying on the parapet above her. He remembered Enos Erb's "Oh, my!" while standing on his tiptoes to see out the office window. And he pictured Aidan Newhouse with handcuffs on one wrist, standing in proud protest at commencement.

"You really do need to stay off campus, Bruce," Branden said. "At least for a while."

Robertson shrugged, saying, "Whatever. Look, Mike. What can you tell me about Ben Capper? Dan's probably going to bring him down to the jail."

Branden said, "He's simple enough—straightforward, I mean. He does a good job as chief of security."

"Does he have a 'thing' for Newhouse?" Robertson asked.

"Like a grudge?"

"Right."

"Not that I know about," Branden said, unhappy to be talking about it.

"He must know how to handle students," Robertson said.

"I guess."

"But professors, Mike—how does he handle them?"

"Newhouse would be a problem for any chief of security, no matter how well he did his job."

"So, why did he put cuffs on the guy?"

"That's a surprise to me," Branden said. "You can't handle an activist like Newhouse with cuffs. He'll just turn it back on you."

"Did they ever have any kind of a run-in, before?" Robertson asked.

Branden checked his watch, tapped his foot. "Not that I know of. If I think of something, I'll let you know."

"In a rush to get somewhere, Mike?"

"Just trying to catch up with Caroline. And I need to ask Cal about that Amish matter."

"Go ahead," Robertson said and ran a flat palm over his gray bristle haircut, blowing out a lungful of consternation. He shook his head and looked back to the ground-level doors into Missy's labs.

"What's the problem?" Branden asked, impatient to leave.

Robertson mumbled, "Don't know, Mike. It's that blond kid's story. I don't buy it."

"Eddie's story? Why not?"

"OK," Robertson said, and lifted his palms in the air to mark a question. "If you're going to graduate on Monday, and you want to have sex with your girlfriend a couple of nights before that, why tell her the next morning that you want to break up? Why not wait until next week, when you'll be a thousand miles away? That'd be less troublesome."

"Maybe he wanted to be forthright with her," Branden said. "Maybe he was showing her respect."

"No," said Robertson confidently. "If it was that, he'd have told her the night before. Before the sex, instead of bedding her on the bell tower. He'd have broken up with her last night, if he wanted to show her respect."

Branden considered that, and said, "He's just a college kid."

"Doesn't fit, Mike," Robertson said. "If he's mean, he'd have waited until Monday, and let commencement separate them. You said it yourself. After commencement, he'll go to Florida, and she'd have gone to Montana. He could have just walked away from her. He wouldn't have had to write to her or return her calls for a while, and he wouldn't have had to break up with her at all. Not face to face, at least."

Surprised by his own indifference, and annoyed at both Robertson and Laughton, Branden checked his watch again. "I'm going to see Caroline. She's over at the church."

"I'm right about your little rich boy, Mike," Robertson said. "The top of that bell tower, after a night of sex, is not where you'd break up with a girl. Not unless you had a heart the size of a chickpea."

Branden took his keys out and said, "Missy will tell you this was a suicide." He got in behind the wheel of his truck, rolled down his window, backed out beside Robertson, and added, "Maybe Eddie

Hunt-Myers is just not very smart with women. Maybe he's stupid about romance."

Robertson laughed. "Right, Mike," he said sarcastically. "Hunt-Myers is stupid about women, and he's the one getting free sex from the girl he plans to dump. That's not stupid, if you ask me. Heartless, but not stupid."

Branden held his foot on the brake. Thought. Put his truck into park, and shut off the engine. "You don't like Eddie's story because, on the one hand, he's too nice, and on the other, he's too mean?"

Robertson said, "A nice guy would have broken up with her the night before. Before the bell tower."

"And the mean guy wouldn't have broken up with her until later? That doesn't wash."

There was silence between the two men for several long seconds, and then Robertson said, "I'm going to interview Eddie myself. See what he knows about women."

Branden smiled and said, "You'll end up talking to his family lawyers."

"Why's that?"

"Because he is Edwin Thomas Hunt-Myers III. He's that 'rich boy' you've been complaining about for most of your life. He's from one of the finest coastal families in south Florida."

"I knew it!" Robertson said, with satisfaction.

"And I knew you'd react this way," the professor said. "You'd have brought him in just for being rich."

"Yeah, well," Robertson said, "now I'm going to bring him in just for being stupid."

7

CAL TROYER'S white board church building was on a hillside in a residential part of Millersburg, south of Jackson Street and east of Clay. Branden passed the tan sandstone courthouse on his way there, and saw Dan Wilsher and Deputy Lance walking into the back of the jail with Ben Capper, who was flushed in the face and animated in speech, though Branden couldn't hear his words.

Branden was weary, spent. Cathy Billett's death weighed on him like the years, and by comparison, the troubles of Enos Erb seemed at first insignificant. But no, Branden thought. That's not right. For an Amishman to have come to him like that . . . He shook his head to free his thoughts and drove on to the church. There he parked beside Caroline's Miata.

The church building was long and narrow, with the sanctuary fronting the parking lot, and the Sunday school classrooms and church offices located at the back. Branden took the walkway down the sunny side of the building and came in through the pastor's office door.

Cal was standing in front of his office window, looking out at the old homes of the neighborhood. His white hair was long, tied in a short tail at the back. The short white bristles of his beard were trimmed to a sharp angle along his chin. He was cleanshaven above his lips, and in this he resembled the Amish. He was dressed in jeans, work boots, and an old blue T-shirt that fit snugly against his stocky torso. His arms were short and powerful, hands big and calloused from his labor as a carpenter. He was not a tall man—a legacy of the genetic heritage of his grandfather's Amish ancestry.

Subdued, Branden said, "Hi, Cal," and looked the pastor over. Without turning from the window, Cal replied only, "Mike."

Branden read tension in the muscles rippling along Cal's forearm. The pastor rolled his shoulders to try to shrug it off.

Seated in a chair in front of Cal's desk, Caroline held up several loose pages of a handwritten letter and an envelope. She handed the envelope to Branden, and the professor read the address:

Pastor Caleb Troyer
Church of Christ, Christian
Millersburg, Ohio 44654

And the return address:

Rachel Ramsayer
112 Henry Street
Montgomery, Alabama 36106

Caroline took the envelope back and handed her husband the letter. It was written in a confident hand with large script letters, in blue ink on bone-white stationery. Branden studied the pastor a moment longer. When the silence continued, he said merely, "Cal?"

The pastor turned at the waist to look at the letter in the professor's hand and then nervously back to the window.

Branden read the letter while standing next to Caroline's chair.

Dear Mr. Troyer,

I apologize ahead of time for the surprise this letter will give you. We have never met, and you'll have no reason to know who I am. Please let me explain. The man who raised me was a cruel drunk who beat me and my mother when it suited him. She divorced him when I was eight years old, and we moved to Alabama. We had been living in Toledo. I've never seen my "father" since, and I have grown accustomed to hating him.

Last November, my mother died of lung cancer. She was a long time dying, and we got a chance to talk about matters. She gave me an envelope to open after her funeral. I thought I knew everything about her. I was wrong.

In her letter to me, she wrote that she was married, briefly, to a soldier. A medic in Vietnam. She met another man, wrote the soldier a "Dear John" letter, and sent him divorce papers through the mail. I have those papers, Mr. Troyer. You signed them in Saigon, in the winter of 1968. She was briefly your wife, but she threw you over for another man, and felt remorse for that the rest of her life. I never knew what caused that underlying sadness in her, but this goes a long way toward explaining it.

In her letter to me, she wrote that you are my real father. I realize that this will be a surprise to you, but I was born nine months after your rotation home on leave, between two tours in Vietnam. You signed the divorce two months after that leave, and my parents were married right after that. But, I was born less than nine months from their marriage, and my "father" knew that I was not his child. I believe that is why he hated us so much.

But, now, Mr. Troyer, my mother has told me that you are my real father. I have had a lot of trouble accepting this. Please don't hate my mother. She was kind and loving to me. She carried heaviness in her heart all her life, I think because of what she did to you.

But, I never knew about any of this. I never knew about you. Not until my mother died. I don't know why she never told me. It would have been a comfort to me to know that the cruel man who raised me was not really my father.

I know this will be a shock to you. I have such an empty hole in my life where you are supposed to be. Do I have any brothers or sisters? Did you ever remarry? Can I come to see you? I have so many questions.

Please write back to me. Please don't be angry with me.

I have checked with the hospital here. If you go to the hospital and let them take a DNA sample (they swab your mouth with a Q-tip), then they can prove that you are really my father. Please do this, Mr. Troyer. Please let me hope that you are my real father.

Sincerely,
Rachel Ramsayer
(Troyer?)

When Branden had finished reading the letter, he handed it back to Caroline and stood silently beside her, waiting for Cal to speak. Cal stood motionless in front of the window and let silence fill the room. When Caroline started to go to him, the professor motioned her gently back into her chair. Cal cleared his throat with difficulty but still held his silence.

Eventually Cal spoke. "I never knew why Sarah wanted the divorce."

The Brandens waited.

"It would have been easier to have known she found someone else," Cal whispered.

Branden asked, "Cal, you never saw Sarah after you came home?"

"No. I let her go. I can't tell you why. She didn't love me—we were just kids."

"What are you going to do, Cal?" Caroline asked.

Prolonged silence followed, with Cal staring out the window. When he finally turned to face them, his eyes were swollen and red, and his cheeks were lined with tears. Caroline got out of her chair and went to embrace him. The professor stood beside them, his hand laid gently on Cal's shoulder.

"I never knew why," Cal whispered.

"She was a fool, Cal," Caroline said. "It's nothing more complicated than that."

Cal said, "A lot of guys got those 'Dear John' letters in Vietnam.

The girls couldn't stand the waiting. They found someone else. She never told me we had a daughter."

Cal dried his cheeks with the backs of his hands. He sat down behind his desk and looked as lost as an abandoned child. He found it hard to look at either of his friends. Mixed with the sadness in his features, the professor read the signs of nervous discomfort, and said, "You don't have to be embarrassed, Cal."

Cal gave a strangled laugh and said, "I know, but I'm in shock. This feels like panic."

The professor glanced at his wife and asked Cal, "What do you want to do?"

"I don't know," said Cal.

"Come out to the house," Caroline said. "We can talk."

"I'm not sure I can. I need time. I need to come at this fresh. Maybe tomorrow."

He needed to let this settle a while. He needed to work on something else, be active, before tackling this challenge. Right now, he needed to sit somewhere and rest his eyes, remembering Sarah as he had known her. "I think I need to be alone," he said, "but I also could use some company. I'm not used to feeling this way."

"Come out to the house later," the professor said. "We'll talk if you like, or we can just sit. I've got an Amish problem for you anyway."

Cal raised his eyebrows and took in a deep breath. "I really don't know what to do."

"Come sit on the back porch," Caroline said. "If you want to talk, we can. In the meantime, I'll make sure Michael doesn't bother you."

That got a weak laugh from Cal. He rose slowly from behind his desk and faced the professor. "You don't look so good yourself," he said.

Branden looked to Caroline and back to Cal. "One of my students killed herself this morning," he said softly. "Jumped off the tower."

"Oh, no!" Caroline cried and leaped to her feet. "Michael!"

Cal's features took a weary sag. "Mike, I'm sorry."

"Cathy Billett," Branden said. "She was in my class this semester. Eddie Hunt-Myers was with her. He's my student, too."

Caroline drew the professor into her arms and held him close, saying, "Michael, are you all right?"

"No," Branden choked.

Cal said again, "Mike, I'm really sorry."

Caroline released her husband, and he stood slumped a little, arms slack at his sides.

Cal said, "I won't bother you now, Mike. Compared to this I don't have a real problem at all."

"Actually, I could use the company," Branden said. "I need to sit by myself a while, but later I could use the company."

Cal studied the professor's eyes and knew not to protest. Rousing himself with difficulty, he asked, "You have an Amish question?"

Branden nodded with a sorrowful smile. "Enos Erb came to my office this morning, just before this happened. He thinks his brother was murdered."

"The dwarves."

"Enos is a dwarf, yes."

Cal said, "So was his brother, Benjamin."

Branden said, "Right. Maybe we can talk about that, Cal. Out at the house, later this afternoon."

8

Friday, May 11
AFTERNOON

AFTER LUNCH at the Brandens', Cal planted himself in a white wicker chair with high armrests on their back porch. He sat there alone much of the remaining afternoon, watching the wind play through the trees at the back edge of the lot. He needed the solitude, and as he watched the trees bend to the weather he let his mind drift on the wind. The spring breeze stiffened gradually and promised rain. Pillow-white clouds grew out of the west and filled the sky. Caroline and the professor gave Cal the solitude he needed to think, and when Caroline once offered coffee, Cal declined.

The professor called Lawrence Mallory and asked him to bring over the essays he needed to grade. When they arrived, he sat in his swivel rocker, staring uselessly at the blue books. Caroline worked at the kitchen table, editing a manuscript for a publisher of children's books.

In midafternoon, Bruce Robertson called to say that Ben Capper had gone back to campus with the promise of forbearance, and that Robertson was going to give "Edwin Hunt-Myers *The All-Mighty* Third" a good going-over about his night on the bell tower with Cathy Billett. He also reported that although Missy Taggert had not yet finished her postmortem exam, there were no preliminary indications that a struggle might have led to Billett's death.

When the doorbell rang, Professor Branden pushed himself wearily out of his chair and answered the door. It was Eddie Hunt-

Myers, dressed in blue slacks, white loafers, and a white Oxford shirt. Without speaking, Branden led Eddie into the living room, and Caroline joined them there. Eddie sat on the edge of the sofa and stared at the carpet. He seemed shut off from humanity, assaulted by an incapacitating mental turmoil that made him incapable of speech.

Caroline asked, "Eddie, can I get you something to drink?"

Eddie shook his head, glanced over at her briefly with an expression of misery, and turned his eyes back to the carpet. She sat next to him on the sofa. He was big beside her, powerful and tanned, but he seemed as helpless as a child.

The professor took a seat opposite them, again in his swivel rocker, and said, "Eddie, I'm sorry, but the sheriff is going to want to talk to you again."

"I don't blame him," Eddie said. He raised his eyes to Branden. "I must be the dumbest man alive. I blame myself. I wish I had jumped, too."

"I wish you wouldn't talk that way, Eddie," the professor said. "I hope you aren't going to do anything rash."

"I can't stop thinking about her, Dr. Branden. I can't get the picture of her out of my mind."

"Eddie," Branden said, "I think you need to talk to someone."

Eddie shook his head, opened his eyes wide with dismay, took a deep breath, and raised his palms as if to say he couldn't make promises about his actions.

Branden said, "Eddie, can you help me understand why you wanted to break up with Cathy?"

With a smile as tragic as his loss, Eddie said, "It wasn't going to work out. There were too many problems."

"Why is that?" Branden asked.

"I'm a bit of a simpleton, Dr. Branden. I know boats, the ocean, harbors, that sort of thing. I work at my parents' boatyard in Florida."

"What's wrong with that?"

"Her folks are big ranchers, Dr. Branden. They want—wanted —Cathy to marry someone with land. Someone who's big into the cattle business. They had a fellow all picked out for her—the boy she dated in high school. Not some dockhand from the south."

"I'm sorry, Eddie," the professor said. "I want to help you."

"It's helping just to know that I can talk to you," Eddie said.

"Come over anytime, Eddie."

"Thanks, Dr. Branden. It'd be nice if I could come over a couple of times this weekend."

"Anytime," Branden repeated.

Eddie nodded his thanks and got up. He looked around the room and said, "It's nice here."

Branden walked him to the door and said, "Call my cell phone if I'm not home, Eddie. You've still got my number?"

"The one in your course syllabus?"

"Right."

Standing at the front door, Eddie put his hand out to shake. The professor accepted his hand and said, "I'll be here grading essays. Come back if you want to talk."

Eddie left struggling to hold back tears.

*   *   *

When the professor had finished reading essays, he penciled a grade on each blue book and set the stack on the coffee table, hoping he'd be able to read the essays again on Saturday, before transmitting course grades to the registrar. Depending on the second reading, two of his students might fail the course. Cathy Billett had earned a B+.

The distraction of grading the essays improved Branden's mood, but he still felt the dismay of loss. He still felt the press of his years. He'd likely change some of those grades once he had a chance to read the exams again. Once his mind was agile again. Still, he was grateful for the familiar task of assessing his students' work. A second time through, and he'd be happier with his work. It would just have to wait a while to get done right.

The professor set his lapboard on the floor, got up, and wandered into the kitchen. Caroline's manuscript sat in a neat stack on the kitchen table. She was working on dinner at the stove and declined his offer to help.

"Go check on Cal, Michael. He's been out there for hours."

Branden crossed through the family room to the back door.

The wind was blowing across the screened porch, and the temperature had dropped. Cal's chair was empty. Branden stepped out onto the long porch and saw Cal standing with his hands stuffed into his jeans pockets, down at the cliff edge of the property. The professor took a seat on the porch.

"Try not to be morose," Branden remembered from Caroline's note that morning. As he watched Cal's white hair dancing with the wind, the professor found that request nearly impossible to honor. He closed his eyes on a scene from his childhood, and saw a youthful Cal Troyer with a fishing rod, on the other side of a bass pond. He saw himself hunting pheasant with Bruce Robertson, along the fence line of a high pasture. And the cases they had worked on together played through Branden's mind—the cases he had worked with Troyer and Robertson over the years, mostly involving the Amish. Most recently, there had been Sarah Yoder's kidnapping, a little less than two years ago.

* * *

When Cal touched Branden's shoulder, the professor's eyes were closed, and his thoughts, though not morose, were not particularly happy. There had been so many years. They had all blown away on the breeze.

Cal said, "You don't look so good," and took a seat beside Branden.

"Time is an enemy, Cal," Branden remarked, true to his mood.

"Time is life," Cal answered. "Death is the enemy."

Branden nodded. "Caroline thinks I've been morose, lately."

"Probably you have."

"Even before this," the professor replied.

Cal asked, "You said you talked with Enos Erb?"

Branden let a silent moment pass and then pulled his thoughts forward. "Yes," he said. "Enos Erb. Why would anyone murder an Amish dwarf?"

"You're not sure anyone did."

"Enos Erb would not have set foot in my office unless he were sure about that."

"There, you are probably right," Cal said. "That congregation at Calmoutier is splitting in half, you know. Families are choosing up sides."

"You knew Benny Erb?" Branden asked.

"Benny, Enos, and Israel. They're all right in the middle of the biggest congregational split in thirty years."

"What's the split over?" Branden asked.

"Science," Cal said. "Specifically, birth defects. More specifically, genetic research. Your Professor Lobrelli wants to develop gene therapy for the Amish—to reverse the damage they've done to themselves through inbreeding. The Amish have more genetic diseases than most people realize, because they marry inside their group. So Enos Erb's district is so divided that brothers and sisters aren't talking to each other anymore. Worse, parents and children."

"Enos didn't mention any of that," Branden said.

"He wouldn't have," Cal said. "He's pro-science. His brother Israel across the road is one of the Antis. Benny was caught in the middle, leaning Pro, but living with Israel. It's a mess."

"How are we going to sort this all out?" asked Branden.

Cal said, "We're not going to. There isn't a sociologist anywhere in the world who'd be able to sort it all out. Families are going to break apart over this. It's real trouble for Amish folk. If you go pro-science—modern—half of the people you know will consider you lost to them. You'd be shunned. So, right now, everybody out there has a decision to make. The Moderns will work for a cure—cooperate with scientists like Lobrelli. They might have to join a Mennonite congregation if they can't organize around their own bishop, but that's what they'll do."

"And the Antis?" Branden asked.

"They'll dig in harder than ever before. It's already tragic, and it's going to get worse."

Branden said, "One of them is dead, Cal. How's it going to get any worse than that?"

Cal said, "Until I opened the mail today, I had no idea I had a daughter. It's a shock. But that's nothing compared to the shock Amish people face when they decide to go modern—when they're shunned."

"Is this split the reason Enos Erb thinks his brother was murdered?"

"I don't know. Amish aren't murderers. But Enos has a real problem—something like what Martin Luther faced when he nailed his *Ninety-five Theses* to the doors of the Wittenberg church."

"I think we should go out there, Cal—go see what this is all about."

"To Calmoutier?"

"Right. Now, if you've got time. But what about your letter, Cal? This Rachel Ramsayer?"

"That's gonna have to wait."

"What if she's really your daughter?"

"I need time, Mike," Cal said, shaking his head. "I'm not ready. Not after all these years."

9

Friday, May 11
4:30 P.M.

MIKE BRANDEN and Cal Troyer drove northeast on State Route 241 to Mt. Hope and then took Mt. Hope Road north to Holmes County 229. At the intersection, there was a single Amish house and the large, open fields of adjoining Amish farms. To the north, the skies were clear, blue, untroubled. To the south there were thunderheads black with turmoil, and lightning flashed along the leading edge, as the storm lumbered toward the east.

Branden turned right onto 229 and followed Troyer's directions east for several miles, past the old St. Genevieve Church, to a flat and straight stretch where two gravel driveways opposed one another on the two sides of the road. A right turn took them to the Enos Erb farm; a left would have taken them to the Israel Erb farm. At the entrance to the right driveway, Enos had posted a hand-lettered sign on a plywood board:

> Beagle Pups—$8
> Trained Rabbit Dogs—$17

Edging 229 and set close to the drive, there was a small red barn with a rusty sheet-metal roof. A slat fence surrounding it enclosed a herd of goats. Two billy goats were tethered outside the fence. Forty yards farther down the gravel lane stood the main house— two stories of white wood frame set on pale yellow foundation blocks, with a wide front porch and a green shingle roof. On the lawn between the big house and the driveway, a young boy and girl, dressed in denim blue and flat black, he in a little straw hat and she in a black bonnet, were playing on a sturdy wooden swing set with a green plastic slide. As the professor's truck approached, the children stopped pumping their little legs and let the swings come to rest. They sat on the swing seats, watching the two English men carefully as Branden and Troyer climbed out of the truck.

Cal called out, "Hi, kids," but they had no words for him. With blank faces, they watched him approach, apparently unwilling to speak either to him or to each other. Cal thought nothing of it, and Branden knew it was typical behavior. Amish children fall silent in the presence of adults, especially English ones.

There was a side door to the house, covered by a slanting roof of green corrugated plastic. Troyer knocked on the screened door there and stepped back a pace. A woman of average height came to the door, recognized Cal, and greeted him through the screen, "Pastor Troyer."

The ties of her white prayer cap fell loosely over her bodice. Her dark green dress brushed her ankles, and her black shoes were laced over black hose.

"Hi, Vera," Cal said. "Is Enos available?"

Vera Erb remained silent while studying the professor, and Cal added, "This is my friend, Vera. Professor Michael Branden."

Vera nodded a modest greeting to Branden and brought her eyes back to Troyer.

"Enos was in town today," Cal said. "He came in to see the professor."

Vera cocked an eyebrow and considered that statement, and Cal realized that she hadn't known about her husband's visit to the professor.

"He's mending tack," Vera said, and tipped her head toward the stables behind the house.

Branden took a step back, turning toward the stables, but Cal held his place in front of the door. Vera stayed put, watching Cal while nervously drying her hands on a towel.

"Are the troubles getting worse, Vera?" Cal asked.

Vera nodded, ill at ease.

Cal said, "Is Enos going to follow the preacher or the bishop?"

Vera said guardedly, "You'd have to ask him, I reckon."

"Is this split a done deal?"

"Folks aren't talking to each other, Cal."

"Israel's still with the Antis?"

"I reckon you'd have to ask him."

"OK, Vera, thanks," Cal said and turned from the door. Branden fell in beside him, and the two walked down the gravel drive, toward the back.

Branden thought it strange to be watched by so many pairs of eyes. Besides the two children on the swings and Vera, who lingered behind the screen, a lad of about fifteen watched through a kitchen window, and two boys who could have been twins stood at the corner of the house, each with a beagle puppy in his arms. Branden nodded a greeting to the two boys as he passed, but got only blank stares. He knew this was their way with strangers, but he figured they must surely know Cal Troyer and ought to give him at least a nod in return. He felt suspect for being English and knew it was more than typical Amish reticence on display here. These boys might very well have good reasons to be suspicious of him. Still, Branden found it unsettling, and it played on his weary emotions. He dropped his eyes from their view.

Behind the big house, the drive angled ninety degrees to the right, skirted the back of the house, and turned south again after thirty yards. Outside this second curve, a Daadihaus sat at the back edge of the main house, on the west side. It was connected to the main house by a trellis-covered walkway.

Across the drive from the Daadihaus stood an open-fronted stable, divided by weathered boards into seven stalls. Enos Erb was in the second stall, where a dozen odd milk crates had been wired together to make a set of steps. Standing on the top level of this makeshift platform, Enos was fitting one of his Belgian draft horses with a new bit and bridle. The horse was bobbing its head, resisting the bit.

The head of the tan and cream Belgian was nearly as big as Enos himself, but he managed to wrestle the bit into place, and the horse settled down. Enos fastened the straps of new leather around the horse's head and saw Troyer and Branden only when he turned to descend his milk crates.

"Stubborn horse," Enos said in his reedy voice. He climbed awkwardly down to ground level and chuckled, "My legs aren't gonna handle these steps much longer. Getting too old."

Cal said, "Hi, Enos," and nodded toward the horse. "You still using Shetler tack?"

"I like 'em good enough," Enos said.

Cal explained for Branden. "The Shetler brothers over south of Fredericksburg make the best leather tack out here."

Enos came forward to offer his hand to Cal and then to the professor. Shyly, he said to Branden, "I wasn't supposed to be on your campus today."

"Do you still want to talk about your brother?" Branden asked.

Enos shrugged in doubt. "I don't really know for sure anymore. I'm not sure what I want. Wouldn't be the first time."

On stiff legs, Enos moved across the drive to a redwood picnic table behind the Daadihaus. He pulled himself up onto the bench on one side and waved Branden and Troyer over to join him. His chin was little more than six inches above the tabletop, and his feet swung free off the ground. Branden and Troyer took seats on the bench opposite him.

Overhead, against moiling clouds and a darkening sky, a dozen purple martins maneuvered like stunt planes, chasing down mosquitoes. In the grass beside the Daadihaus, a young girl played with beagle puppies in a cardboard box. Three older boys and a girl hoed quietly in a large vegetable garden behind the stables. From a larger barn behind the garden came the ping of a hammer striking metal. There were children's shouts and the banging of screened doors, as several kids ran into and out of the house in a game of tag. Vera Erb came out after the youngsters and scolded them mildly in German dialect, and the children filed back into the house, teasing and pinching one another once their mother's back was turned. Lightning flashed to the south, and several seconds later, there was a thunderous rumbling on the horizon.

Enos watched the children and remarked with obvious satisfaction, "Only one of my children is going to be short—a dwarf like me. We've got nine. Professor Lobrelli says that's not too bad with the odds—one dwarf in nine."

Cal asked, "How well do you know Lobrelli?"

"Good enough, I suppose," said Erb. "She works on blood—the blood science."

Branden asked, "Do you go in to see her? Go in to the college, I mean?"

"No. She came out to ask us questions a couple of times. Plus she came out when her scholars helped her take our blood. Mostly we talk to the scholars, now."

"You mean her students?" Branden asked.

"Students—scholars, yes. The college students. They're the ones who took our blood. And they come out to talk."

"Did they do that a lot around here?" Cal asked. "Take blood samples?"

"From those who'd allow it," Enos said.

"Your whole family?" Cal asked.

"Yep. But not Israel's. He's against science."

"How about Benny?" Branden asked.

"You mean give his blood?"

"Right."

"Well, he did, yes, but he never told anyone."

"Benny was modern?" Cal asked. "He went against Israel?"

"Not so's Israel would know," Erb said.

Branden asked, "Does anyone in Israel's family think science is good?"

"Nope. He doesn't—they don't. They're all staying with the bishop."

Branden asked, "It's your bishop who's an Anti?"

"He's the leader," Erb said with a distasteful expression.

"Andy Miller?" Cal asked.

"Yes. Andy Miller. He's asked John Hershberger to take all the modern people and go."

"So that's the split, then," Branden said. "Over Lobrelli's research. Over genetic research."

"Blood research," Enos explained. "She thinks the dwarfism is in our blood. She thinks we give it to our children through our blood."

"Makes sense," Cal said. "The genes are in the blood. The DNA tests can trace a genetic defect, if they know the markers to look for."

Enos nodded with the assurance of someone familiar with science. "She has her scholars ask us a lot of questions about genealogy— those of us who'll talk about it, anyway. She has the whole clan mapped out on a chart in her office. And the blood is what she works on in her laboratory."

"That's pretty modern, Enos," Cal said. "I'm surprised any Amish are cooperating at all."

"Preacher Hershberger says it doesn't make any sense that we'd use Saint-John's-wort to pick up a mood and not be willing to take modern drugs for depression. He says it's the same thing, only better, and we've been using herbs for centuries."

Cal nodded agreement.

Branden asked, "Was Benny depressed?"

"Not Benny!" Erb said. "He was the happiest man I know. A real chatterbox."

"So he would have talked to Lobrelli?" Branden asked.

"Benny talked to everyone," Enos said. "He went to town any chance he got. Down to Mt. Hope, and Millersburg too. He'd sit down at the courthouse and talk to people. That's how Lobrelli got to know us all out here—through Benny the chatterbox."

"Did Andy Miller go against Benny, too?" Cal asked.

"He's the bishop," Enos said simply, as if the answer would be obvious. "He's against just about anything that's modern—science most of all."

The wind took a chill, and pulled at Erb's beard. The storm seemed to be easing northward to find them. Erb ignored a flash of lightning. He let his thoughts wander over a memory, and the distraction showed in his eyes.

Cal noticed and asked, "Have you thought of something, Enos?"

"I was thinking Andy Miller should understand better," Enos said. "He should understand about medicine better, because his own daughter died of the shakies two years ago."

"Parkinson's Disease?" Branden asked.

"Don't know," Erb said. "Her hands shook so bad she couldn't feed herself. Professor Lobrelli says that's in the blood, too."

"It's genetic," Cal said.

"Yes. Genetics in the blood. That's what Benny and I have. Lobrelli said we got it from our ancestors."

"You said Benny was happy and talkative," Branden said.

Enos nodded, "Benny liked everyone. He was a favorite with the children out here. He'd play with them."

"Was he backward?" Cal asked. "Childlike?"

"You mean dumb?"

Cal flushed a little red in the cheeks and nodded.

"No," Erb said, unconcerned. "Benny was smart, normal. And happy. Just is, see, he didn't have average height."

Cal sat drumming his thumbs on the picnic table. "You're talking about a big difference, Enos, between the Moderns and the Antis. Benny would have had to move off Israel's farm if it came to a head. He'd have had to move."

"Israel wouldn't have asked him to move," Enos said confidently. "He needed Benny to run the store."

"Benny died in the store," Troyer explained for Branden.

"Right," Enos said. "A couple of weeks ago. They say he fell off a ladder, but I don't believe it."

Branden and Troyer waited for an explanation.

"Calcification."

"What?" Branden asked.

"Benny's legs were stiff like mine, only worse. Calcification. His knees and hips were going bad. He waddled like a duck because he couldn't bend anymore."

"He was having trouble walking?" Cal asked.

"Right, worse than me. That's why Israel and Bishop Miller ought to know not to be so Anti. They ought to let people try the new medicines."

The dark clouds behind them seemed to edge a boundary between danger and safe haven, blue skies to the north, angry skies to the south. The wind shifted and brought occasional drops of rain, large and powerful when they struck, as if they had fallen from an improbable height.

Branden asked, "Would you have taken Benny in over here?" and turned on his seat to eye the clouds coming in low.

"We talked about that."

"And?"

"Benny didn't want to disappoint Israel. So he kept his ideas to himself over there."

This time Branden held the pause. The wind slapped cold against his back, and he felt exposed. He pushed the storm out of his mind and thought of Benny with his stiff legs. "Benny couldn't climb ladders anymore," he mused.

"Right!" Enos said. "So how'd he break his neck by falling off of one?"

10

Friday, May 11
5:35 P.M.

THE PROFESSOR and the pastor were just approaching the college when they heard coming from the campus the deep thumping of a bass and the riffs of a Jimi Hendrix guitar solo in "Hey Joe." The classic rock and roll song about murder, it was immediately followed by Jefferson Airplane's "Somebody to Love."

When Branden turned onto his street, the storm had passed, and the pavement was littered with branches and leaves blown from the trees. The evening air was cold, and the tree limbs hung low, heavy with strain. Branden's tires hissed through a puddle at the corner, and when he made the turn, he saw Caroline standing out on the pavement of the cul-de-sac in front of their house, listening to the music two blocks away. They came up to her with the windows down, and she said, "It's starting all over again, Michael. It's that same music again. It's Vietnam all over again."

The professor said, "Hang on," and parked his truck on the curb.

Caroline and the two men walked toward campus. When they got to the dripping oak grove, they found twenty or thirty students and a few older professors marching in a loose circle in front of the stone chapel, around a mound of flowers, balloons, stuffed animals, and cards heaped on the spot where Cathy Billett had died. A scrawny student with a scruffy black beard was loading another

CD into a changer. Two large theater speakers stood next to the CD player in the grass. A yellow electric cable with a long extension cord snaked up to a socket set into the foundation stones of the chapel. The mourners had trampled the cable where it crossed the stone walkway, so another student in tattered jeans and a tie-dyed T-shirt was trying to fasten the cable to the wet stone with a roll of duct tape marked "Sociology Department."

Troyer and the Brandens stood back thirty yards from the procession and watched. The next song to play was Peter, Paul, and Mary's recording of "Blowin' in the Wind," and Cal asked Branden, "Where'd these kids learn about all the old songs?"

Branden gave a short laugh, and said, "Newhouse teaches a seminar on the sixties. It's the most popular class on campus."

"How many take it?"

"About half."

"So Newhouse has a ready-made protest march, any time he wants one."

"Pretty much," Branden said. "He's had groups down at the courthouse several times this semester. Says it's part of his class."

Aidan Newhouse marched proudly, carrying a tall candle. From his right wrist dangled the silver handcuffs that Ricky Niell had tried to remove. At intervals, Newhouse urged his marchers on. When he saw Mike Branden he waved and stuck his manacled wrist into the air like a badge of honor.

Branden smiled at Newhouse and shook his head. Newhouse was simply obeying his essential nature. He could not have resisted this theater's stage any more than he could have voted for Reagan.

Newhouse pointed off to the right, and when Branden looked in that direction, he saw Chief of Security Ben Capper standing alone at the far edge of the grove, in the shadow of the history building. He pointed him out to Cal and Caroline, remarking, "Ben Capper fought in Vietnam."

Cal nodded, eyes fixed on the chief of security.

Caroline said, "Aidan's going to wear those cuffs to commencement, isn't he?"

Ruefully, the professor said, "We'll be lucky if he's out of them by fall semester."

"Let's get out of here," Cal said, but then stopped. "Wait," he said, and pointed back to Capper.

Chief of Security Ben Capper walked up slowly to the memorial that had been laid down for Cathy Billett, and he squeezed through and stood in the middle of the circle of mourners. The marching stopped momentarily, but Aidan Newhouse said, "Keep marching," and the little crowd started circling around Capper.

Capper stood motionless for several turns of the circle, and then he bent over and picked up a brown teddy bear with a yellow ribbon tied around its neck. His eyes sought out Newhouse in the crowd, and he asked, "Do they even know what a yellow ribbon means?"

Newhouse thrust his manacled wrist into the air over his head and kept marching silently.

Capper laid the stuffed bear back on the memorial pile and squeezed through the circle of people again, coming out on the side near Troyer and the Brandens. Spotting them, he walked over to them wearily.

"Mike," he said in greeting. "Cal. Mrs. Branden. I don't think these kids even know what a yellow ribbon signifies."

Cal said, "You served in Vietnam."

"Air Cav. I flew Hueys."

Cal said, "Medical Corps."

"You know Newhouse has led Iraq war protest marches down at the courthouse?" Capper asked.

Cal nodded and said gently, "I think he's got a point, Ben."

Capper nursed his antagonism while he considered that statement. Making an obvious effort to contain his anger, he said, "Nam makes us brothers, Cal. You and I are not going to have an argument over Iraq."

Cal offered his hand, and Capper took it forcefully. He pulled Cal to himself and embraced him. Then he turned and walked out of the oak grove, head high, shoulders back, fists clenching and releasing at his sides.

*　*　*

Once they got home, Caroline put on a pot of coffee and sat at the kitchen table with her husband and the pastor. While the coffee maker chirped, she traced the grain in the curly maple tabletop with her finger and gave a little nervous shudder. "Newhouse knows the police were as much a problem to the marchers in the sixties as the war was," she said. "He's going to wear those cuffs every day now, and he's going to try to bring it all back. He's been waiting for something like this all his life."

Cal said, "It's not the same. This is not about racism, or society, or free love. It's not anything like that this time. Now, it's all about the war in Iraq. That's where Newhouse will take this."

The professor said, "You'd think so, Cal, but I promise you Newhouse isn't that big a thinker. He's not going to do anything that'll quench his glory, and that has always been teaching about the sixties."

Cal barked out a "Humpf" as protest.

Branden said, "He's the real deal, Cal. A true McGovern believer. A Woodstock idealist. He's never harmed anyone, and he won't try to make this any bigger than it is."

"He's exploiting Cathy Billett's death to make a political point," Caroline complained.

"It's more about the handcuffs," Branden said. "He was handled roughly by police in a southern protest march in the sixties, and he spent nearly twenty-four hours chained to an iron bar in the basement of a horrid little jail. He doesn't like handcuffs, and if Ben and Ricky hadn't used any today, this would all have blown over. It would never have gotten started."

"So, you don't object?" Cal asked.

"Not to Newhouse, I don't," Branden said. "He's always been forthright about his beliefs, and when we talk about the issues of the sixties, he is logical, measured, and fair. He's a debater, Cal. He'll debate it as long as he can talk. But do any harm to someone? No. Aidan Newhouse is too much of a peace advocate to ever contemplate violence."

"Then what?" Cal asked. "What's he want?"

"It's going to stay local. It's all about the handcuffs. Ben Capper is just the kind of person Aidan Newhouse most distrusts. He distrusts that type of authority. He's going to go after Ben Capper. He's going to try to get him fired."

"And if he can't hurt Ben?" Caroline asked.

"He'll try to take down somebody for allowing this to happen. Maybe Arne Laughton."

"The president?" Cal asked.

"Right. Arne Laughton kicked Professor Aidan Newhouse's son out of college about ten years ago, for cheating on his senior research project."

11

Friday, May 11
8:30 P.M.

WHEN MIKE BRANDEN drove Cal Troyer home, he parked in the church lot next door to Cal's small house, and he shut the engine down intending to sit a while and talk. It was a cool night, damp from the storm, but they had the windows of the truck rolled down. Cal eased back in the passenger's seat and hung his elbow out the window. "I don't know, Mike," he sighed, eyes turned away. "Enos only has vague suspicions. I think it's pretty thin. Maybe Benny tried to go up the ladder and failed. You'd just be meddling."

Branden arched his back and rubbed at tension in his shoulders. The Cathy Billett tragedy had lodged as a sharp complaint in his muscles, and he was having trouble thinking about Benny Erb. But it was more than that. In his living room, he had watched remorse nearly cripple Eddie Hunt-Myers, as he explained to Branden why he had tried to tell Cathy they shouldn't be together anymore. And then there was his job. Maybe he'd handle this better if he weren't so sick of grading papers, he thought. Maybe he'd be less of a useless complainer if he could just do his job like everyone else. But that was the trouble—it was just a job to him, now. It was just a way to make money. His disaffection toward what had once been a career was hurting him. And he'd always promised himself that if it ever came to that, he'd retire. So, put up or shut up, Professor, he told himself. And then there was Benny Erb.

"Maybe Enos didn't tell us everything, Cal. I don't think his brother Israel would be strong on the Anti side without a good reason. There must be something else mixed in here."

"Amish are a suspicious lot," Cal argued. He felt restless and annoyed, nervous about the letter on his desk.

"Still," Branden said.

"OK, then how do you plan to investigate?" Cal asked. His mind was working on the Rachel Ramsayer problem, not really on Benny Erb.

"I'll talk to Israel."

"He might not let you," Cal argued.

"Then I'll go into his little store. At least I can have a look around. See this ladder Enos is talking about."

"Won't be able to see anything," Cal said, an unusual impatience in his tone.

"You could introduce me to some of the people in Andy Miller's district."

"Don't know 'em all," Cal said dismissively.

"Introduce me to this Bishop Miller, then," Branden said, thinking Cal a bit terse.

There was no answer from Cal.

The lamps of the church parking lot painted faint yellow light into the cab of the truck. A cool, damp breeze drifted in through the windows. Cal sat with his thoughts hidden, and Branden wondered why the pastor seemed so reluctant to talk.

"What are you going to do about your letter, Cal?"

"Don't know."

"You could write back. Take it slow."

"I don't know, Mike, OK?" There was frustration in his words.

Branden ignored it. "OK, Cal. At least call her up. Take the DNA test. Move it forward, somehow."

"I can't get past her mother."

"That's not like you, Cal."

"Yeah? Well," Cal said, with bitterness fringing his delivery.

Branden held silence, surprised by Cal's sarcasm.

"It's too much, Mike. It's too much to handle all at once."

Branden turned in his seat and saw Cal's familiar profile, silhouetted by lamplight, and he marked the years in Cal's face. He saw a hollow aspect there, framed by consternation. The young Cal Troyer Branden had known in grade school was hidden underneath the years, now. And there was doubt in Troyer's eyes, something the professor had rarely seen there.

"You going to be OK?" the professor asked softly.

Cal shrugged, looked over briefly, and popped the door handle. He swung his feet out, paused, and asked, "What are you going to do about Lobrelli? She's mixed into this, you know."

"That's where I'll start, Cal. Tomorrow."

12

MIKE BRANDEN found Professor Nina Lobrelli the next morning in a large office adjoining her labs in the new science building, on the opposite side of the stone chapel from the history building. Parked in front of a large desk cluttered with manuscripts and journals, Lobrelli was staring so intently at her laptop that she didn't notice Branden in her doorway until he cleared his throat. She looked up briefly, saying, "One minute, Mike." After saving a file, she pushed back from her desk and added, "Sending an e-mail to all of my students."

"About Cathy?" Branden asked.

Lobrelli nodded. "I want to spend some time with my research students and teaching assistants, to help all of us get through this. Truth is, though, I don't know how I'll get through this myself. I'm in shock. I can't believe she's really gone."

"Cathy was one of your assistants?"

"Teaching assistant, Mike. In my sophomore-level genetics class. But she started a research project last summer and was going to finish it for her senior thesis, next year."

Lobrelli stayed seated at her desk. She sighed. She looked at Branden with a question in her eyes and said, "Why don't you have a seat, Mike? She was your student, too."

Branden stayed on his feet and said, "She was in my Civil War class. So was her boyfriend Eddie."

Lobrelli shook her head with a leaden slowness and dropped her eyes to her desk. Without looking up, she said, "Cathy was going to defy her parents. She was going to follow Eddie home to Florida, after he graduated."

"She must have loved him," Branden said.

"They loved each other, Mike. He's devastated."

"You've talked with Eddie?"

"Earlier this morning. He's trying to write a letter to the Billetts."

"What would he say to them?" Branden asked.

"That's the problem—he doesn't know. But he thinks he owes them a letter, and he came here to ask me about that."

"What did you tell him?"

"That it would be a very difficult letter to write, and get it right."

"No kidding," Branden said. "How do you know Eddie?"

"He took my genetics class last year, but he also wrote his senior thesis for Aidan Newhouse, upstairs in the psychology labs. I was his second reader when he defended, and his thesis was so good that I nominated it for the OPA Walton Prize."

Branden did not recognize the prize, and Lobrelli surmised as much, saying, "It's the Ohio Psychological Association. The Walton is their top scholarly prize, Mike. I think he's got a lock on it. Eddie, I mean. His thesis is worthy of a master's degree."

Branden said, "I know he's smart, Nina. He just earned an A in my Civil War class. But I didn't know his senior thesis was that good. I hadn't heard about your having nominated it."

"Nominations are going to be announced in OPA's journal, in the June issue. I just told Aidan about that last week." Lobrelli shut down her laptop and asked, "So what's up, Mike? What can I do for you?"

Branden said, "I'm here for a lesson, Nina. On another matter."

"Oh?"

"Biochemistry."

"That's a big subject," Lobrelli said. She rose from her chair, stepped around to the side of her desk, and pulled a thick volume off her shelf. When she handed it to Branden, its weight tugged at his arms.

He hoisted it back, and Lobrelli laughed when she took it. "That's just an introductory text," she said.

Professor Lobrelli was dressed as always in jeans and a simple button-front blouse under a tattered white lab coat, which she wore perpetually, even to lectures. She wore a broad smile most of the time and spoke with a Carolina accent. Her eyes were a soft brown, but there hadn't been a student who had mistaken her for soft in over a decade. She had always impressed Branden with her success at writing proposals for federal or private funding of her research, and she was one of only a few professors at Millersburg College who devoted themselves to undergraduate research during the summers. It was common knowledge that any bright student with ambition and a good work ethic could start a research project with her as a sophomore and finish senior year with at least one publication in a professional journal.

Lobrelli sat back against the edge of her desk. "You never come visiting, Mike," she said.

"There's never enough time."

"You hear about Newhouse?" she asked.

"I was there when Cathy Billett died. I saw his marchers yesterday."

"You saw her jump, Mike?"

"No, but I saw her on the stone walkway before the paramedics took her away."

"Do you know if her parents are here?" Lobrelli asked.

"Arne says they're flying into Cleveland this morning."

"That's going to be rough, Mike. Arne's not so good with this sort of thing."

Branden showed Lobrelli a deep scowl. "I had to convince him to call her parents, yesterday afternoon."

"Oh?"

"He was on the phone with Eddie Hunt-Myers's father."

Lobrelli shook her head. She folded her arms over her chest and changed the subject. "Ben Capper's not so bright."

"It's Aidan Newhouse we need to worry about," Branden said. "He's gonna milk this."

"Capper should have known that."

Branden said, "Right. You're right."

"A hundred bucks says he'll still be in those cuffs for commencement."

"I'll pass," said Branden, laughing.

Lobrelli shrugged and changed the subject back to Branden's visit. "Why the interest in biochemistry, Mike?"

"You're doing genetics with some Amish people. How's that working out?"

Lobrelli started right in on the science, pulling Branden over to her chalkboard. She drew a circle and then a square, and connected the two with a wavy line. "We study transcriptional activators, Mike," she said. "If this square represents an activation domain, or AD, and the circle represents a DNA binding domain, DBD, then we want to find compounds that will either enhance binding to DNA or enhance transcriptional activity. We're looking for the kinds of artificial activators that could one day reverse a genetic disorder. Right now we're working with isoxazolidines . . . "

Branden stopped her with a palm in the air. "You lost me with transcriptional."

Lobrelli seemed puzzled, distressed to think that her drawing had not been clear.

"It's the Amish," Branden said. "How are the Amish involved?"

"Well, they're not, really," Lobrelli said, and erased her drawing slowly.

"You've taken blood samples?" Branden asked. "It's genetic research?"

"Well, the blood samples aren't part of our main research,

really," Lobrelli said. "I've got some students who are tagging blood samples for recessive genes, and Amish prove to be good subjects for that, but it's not part of my research. It's a student-initiated project, really. Cathy Billett was in charge of it, as my teaching assistant. I made it available as extra credit in my genetics class."

"Why the Amish?" Branden asked.

"They intermarry," Lobrelli said.

"And that's something that causes a genetic problem," Branden said.

"Right. So we map that with our blood samples and our genealogy charts."

Branden hesitated, perplexed by the discrepancy between her account and Erb's. "You're not looking for a cure?"

"No, it's just research, Mike. Even if we found a perfect transcriptional RNA activator, it wouldn't reverse anyone's symptoms. We're not medicinal here."

"But you are studying genetics for the Amish, looking for a cure," Branden said.

"We just do the fundamental science, Mike, on isoxazolidines. It's strictly laboratory research—biochemistry. You know, the transcriptional activators. The cures come later. We always explain that to them when the Amish ask about it. That the drug companies might come up with a cure farther down the line. On the side, then, I also have my genetics class mapping genetic disorders by taking blood samples and investigating genealogy. But that's jut a class project, designed to enhance their educations. Nothing will ever really come of it."

"And Cathy Billett was in charge of that?" Branden asked.

"As my teaching assistant, yes."

"In the genetics class. OK. And that's separate from your research?"

"Very much so, Mike. We do fundamental research, in our laboratories. The drugs may become available fifteen to twenty years down the road, but that's not guaranteed."

"I'm not sure they get it, Nina. I think some Amish people expect you to develop gene therapy for them. You know—a new drug, right now."

Lobrelli shook her head vigorously. "Let me show you my latest grant proposal."

"No," Branden said and laughed. "I'm not the one for that. I'm curious, though, how you got Amish people to cooperate with you."

"Oh," Lobrelli said, disappointed not to be able to explain her research. "OK, well, I got to know a fellow because he was working with Aidan on a psychology project. Upstairs. He does his interviews on the second floor."

"A dwarf?" Branden asked.

"Yes, but he died."

"Benny Erb."

"Yes, Benny," Lobrelli said. "I met him in Aidan's office one day. Benny asked me about my research."

"So, Benny Erb was your first contact."

She nodded. "I got the idea that we'd do some gene mapping of the population. You know—incident rates for certain genetic disorders. Benny was a dwarf, so that's where it started. Dwarfism is a common genetic disorder among Amish people."

Branden said, "His brother is a dwarf, too."

"I know," Lobrelli said. "Enos."

Branden thought for a moment, hesitated, and asked, "Did you uncover other disorders?"

"Why are you interested?" Lobrelli asked.

"I've gotten to know Enos a little," Branden said.

Lobrelli said, "Well, there's a rare skin disorder in Holmes County."

"Anything else?"

"Parkinson's," Lobrelli said. "At twice the national rate."

"But there's medicine for that," Branden observed. "I've read about that."

"L-DOPA, Mike. It's effective, if you take it on a regular basis. If you start early."

"What about Amish who spurn medicines like that?"

"It'd cut their survival rates in half."

"And you're not developing medicine?" Branden asked. "Not really doing medical research?"

"We do basic science, here, Mike. I let the big companies figure out the drugs."

13

Saturday, May 12
10:20 A.M.

PROFESSOR BRANDEN drove out to the Erb farms near Cal-moutier and turned left onto the Israel Erb property. Immediately to his left, he found a gravel parking lot in front of a small grocery store with red board siding. He pulled into the lot and parked.

The building was old, with small black metal push-tilt windows on the front. He found the single wooden door locked. The windows were pushed out and open. Looking in, he found it was dark and silent inside.

Behind the store, Branden followed a narrow concrete sidewalk that angled across the drive to a large main house of brown brick, standing two and a half stories high over a weathered stone foundation. The concrete walkway took him along the west side of the house to a back porch in the angle created by a wood frame addition that was fully a third the size of the main house. On the back of the addition, there were two smaller structures attached in sequence, with little covered porches in front of matching single doors. Each appeared to be an apartment no larger than a sitting room.

Branden mounted the steps to the back porch and knocked on the screened door. He got no answer. There was light from several lamps inside the house. Past drawn purple curtains, a movement caught the corner of his eye. But no one came to the door.

The family garden on the other side of the drive was situated behind the grocery store. There was no one working in the garden. No kids playing in the yard. There was no workaday noise on the farm, he realized. No lawn mowers growling, no buggies moving, no work at all. On an Amish farm as large as this, there should have been activity. Instead it was as still as a prayer.

Pushing aside a mounting unease, Branden reasoned that someone must be inside. He tried another knock on the back door. He got no response.

Back in his truck, Branden crossed Nisley Road to the Enos Erb farm. On the gravel drive by the main house, two older Amish men in a conservative black buggy had pulled up to Enos, who was standing on the front lawn, with his eyes cast to the ground at his feet. Branden stopped his truck a dozen yards back and switched off the engine. The older of the two men in the buggy looked straight ahead, neither talking to Erb nor acknowledging him. The other man spoke to Erb in a stern and authoritative voice, in the low Dietsche dialect of the county.

Enos Erb looked as miserable as a scolded child, but the stern man kept talking, unconcerned about the dwarf's embarrassment. Next to the buggy, Enos was childlike in size. Even a man of average height would have been mortified, Branden judged, to be spoken to in this fashion by a man sitting so imposingly far above him. Enos no doubt was stricken.

The men in the buggy bore the attitude and posture of leaders accustomed to steadfast obedience. They were evidently habituated to accepting the rightfulness of stern decisions and commands. To accepting the rightfulness of harsh measures and absolute authority. And Enos Erb appeared to Branden to be completely overwhelmed by their words.

When the two men had finished talking to Erb, the elder of the two whipped the horse to a labored gait that took them past the professor quickly. Neither of the men acknowledged Branden, who pulled his truck forward as Enos was climbing the steps to his front porch. He got out of his truck just as Enos reached up to open the front door, and by the way the dwarf's hand hesitated on the doorknob, Branden knew that Enos was aware of him. Branden used that awkward pause to ask, "Enos, where's your brother? Where's his family? What's happening?"

Enos held himself motionless in front of the door for a long five seconds, with his back to the professor, head bowed. Then he went inside without turning around or giving an answer, and Professor Branden found himself standing alone on a second farm that had fallen completely silent. Looking nervously around, he sought the normal—a buggy rolling on the drive, kids working or playing, a daughter hanging clothes on a line, a son chopping wood, the ping of a hammer against metal, the whinny of a horse—and found none of it. Instead he heard the silence of mourning—the mute intensity of the dead. It would have made sense to him only if the windows had been draped in black for a funeral.

Behind him, a woman said, "They're not coming out, Professor."

He turned to see a dowdy woman approaching across the lawn on awkward legs. She had puffy cheeks and fat arms. She was dressed in a faded red dress and a light blue, waist-length windbreaker. Her white knee stockings had bunched at her ankles, and her hair was a matching ultra white. She was shaking her head.

"That was the bishop, Professor," she said and stuck out her hand. "He's laid down the law, for sure."

Branden took her hand and said, "You know me but . . ."

"'But I don't know you,'" the woman interrupted, finishing his sentence for him. "I'm the neighbor, Willa Banks."

Branden held her hand for a moment, released it, and said, "Then you know me because of . . ."

"Pictures in the paper," Willa finished for him.

A sentence finisher, Branden thought. "Then that was . . ." he led.

"The bishop, Andy Miller, of course, I already told you that. He had his little toady Eli Mast with him."

"And the preachers in the district are . . ." Branden started.

"Toady Mast, for one," Willa said. "Preacher number two is John Hershberger. He's splitting off a group of Moderns over the question of medicine."

"Andy Miller asked him to leave the congregation?"

"Better off!" Willa sang. "Andy Miller is as close to those dirty Schwartzentrubers as you can get and still buy your groceries at a market."

Branden stated, "You don't like him very much."

"Can't stand him!" Willa spat. "He's got poor little Enos so flabbergasted that he can't tend his farm. They're all holed up in there, you can believe that. And the same across the way."

Branden waited, figuring he'd get more.

Willa Banks stood on the lawn in front of the Enos Erb farm-house and started right in on the bishop, wagging a finger at Branden. "Miller has been going around to all the Moderns, telling them that they'll be excommunicated if they side with Preacher Hershberger. He's got Enos so worked up I think he's gonna pop a cork. There's families all up and down this road who have got to decide—and I mean right now—whether to stay with Andy Miller and Toady Mast, or go with Hershberger."

Branden looked off in the direction from which Willa had come, and he said, "Your place is . . ."

"Next door, Professor. Right next door. They're all so secretive and all, these Amish, and they think nobody out here can see what's really going on. And that Miller lost a daughter to Parkinson's. Because he wouldn't pay for medicine, the cheap, miserable puke! Pardon my French."

Branden started walking toward Willa Banks's property. As she turned to walk with him, he said, "Enos is a Modern. Israel is Anti . . ."

"And that's going to be real trouble," Banks said, and fell in beside the professor.

Walking slowly, Branden said, "Israel's place is all closed up, too."

Willa laughed coarsely. "Not his store, I'll bet."

The professor did not correct her.

Banks walked him through a narrow stand of trees dividing the properties and came out the other side in a field of strawberries. Here, she guided the professor around the perimeter, saying, "I let the Erb children pick strawberries. Brings in a few bucks each year."

They walked the edge of the field fronting Nisley Road and came up to Willa Banks's double garage of corrugated aluminum. She led him around to the front door of a battered double-wide trailer, faded green on the outside and furnished in an outdated orange and brown "modern" style from the fifties. Before he could take the place in, Branden found himself planted deep in a sticky upholstered chair that might have been salvaged from a dumpster. The little living room where he sat was as dingy and tattered as the old rug at his feet. The color scheme was numbingly consistent. What wasn't orange was brown. Even the shades on the table lamps were yellowed by age to a disconcertingly dirty brown hue. The professor found himself thinking of a shower. Thinking of burning his clothes. Maybe a treatment for lice.

Willa stepped behind a curtain and came out to hand Branden a can of beer. She popped the top on her own can and drank eagerly before wiping the back of her hand across her lips. Branden's every instinct was to pry himself off the cloying fabric of the chair and find his way back to his truck. But something kept him pinned where he sat. As he struggled to understand what that was, he reminded himself of the silence. It was the same complete silence at both farms. Perhaps it was the silence of fear. Or it could have been the silence of withdrawal—something that Bishop Miller would require of his people. A silence of pulling inward for safety from the English, in general terms, but was it something else?

"The two little cousins know better than all of them," Willa said, breaking into his thoughts. "They sneak over here to play."

Branden waved Willa Banks to a chair and took a polite sip of his beer.

Willa asked, "You a biochemist, too, like Lobrelli?"

"No, I'm in history," Branden said. "You know Nina?"

"Not really, but I've heard a lot about her."

"From . . ." Branden led.

"From her students, of course. They all come to see me eventually, on account of I know the scene out here. I know all the kids, all the teenagers, all the parents, and more. Been here thirty-three years. Right here in this trailer. Sooner or later, all those college kids figure out that they have to talk to me to find out what's really going on."

Branden asked, "And what were you saying about two cousins?"

"Albert and Mattie?"

"You tell me, Willa."

"Albert Erb is four years old, maybe four and a half now. He's Israel's kid. Mattie is five, and she's Enos Erb's kid. They've been playing together while all this split-up has been going on, so I figure they know better behavior than all the grown-ups do! Hah! How do you like that, Professor?"

Branden saluted her knowledge with a nod. "So, naturally, you know all about Albert and Mattie?"

"Naturally," Willa said, and drank long from her can of beer.

"Can you tell me about it?" Branden asked. He took another sip.

"Little Albert Erb crosses the road when his mother's not looking, and he waits in those woods we crossed through. Then his little cousin Mattie comes out of Enos's house and meets him there. They play in my woods out back, almost every day. They've got themselves a couple of beagle puppies."

"And they're not supposed to do that?" Branden asked.

"Oh, no. Not at all, Professor. Israel is an Anti. He put a stop to those two playing together when Enos declared himself for the Moderns."

"But you let them sneak over here?"

"What's to let, Professor? They're only four and five, and it's a free country, last I checked."

It didn't make sense, Branden thought. Bishop Miller was Old Order Amish and extremely autocratic, but even the Schwartzentrubers would have talked to him, if he had showed up and knocked on their door. Amish people weren't dug in like the Branch Davidians. They participated in society. They went to town markets. They stopped to talk with strangers. Israel should have come to the door. Enos should at least have turned around to speak with him.

But it had been the same at Israel's farm as it was at Enos's. These two families were barricaded in their houses, not even answering the door. And the store Israel ran? That was locked, contrary to Willa Banks's intuition.

So the split in Andy Miller's district wasn't the crisis that had caused Enos to rebuff him on the porch. The new bishop wasn't just telling his people to withdraw from the world. There was something else behind this silence.

Willa watched him think it through and said, "If you want to know what's going on out here, you need to talk to some of the kids."

Branden asked, "Are Mattie and Albert over here, now?"

Willa finished her beer, crushed it flat on the coffee table, and said, "Naw. They're probably back home by now."

The professor eased out of Willa's disgusting chair and said, "Willa, can you show me? Show me where they play?"

* * *

They skirted the south edge of the strawberry patch and entered the woods on a little trail. The path was difficult to see, so Branden allowed Banks to lead and followed her deeper into the trees. As soon as they were out of sight of her trailer, they found a little shoe.

Farther down the winding trail they found a boy's denim waistcoat. Willa gave it a puzzled look.

The trail crested a ridge and dropped at an angle down to a stream. There a knit skull cap was floating in a pool, and Branden charged ahead.

On the other side of the stream, the trail rose again, and halfway up the other side, Branden, leading by twenty yards now, found more boy's clothes scattered on the ground, next to a tangle of black hair.

Near the hair lay battery-powered hair clippers, half buried in the leaves. Banks bent over to pick up the clippers, but Branden said, "No, Willa. Better leave that."

And then they heard a muffled whimper.

On the other side of an oak tree the size of a house, he found a small Amish girl, bound and gagged. Fully clothed but dirty, she lay prone, struggling against her bindings. Her brow was streaked with blood, some of it having run into her eyes, and her hands were stained with a terrifying crimson.

When she saw Branden, the little girl froze her eyes on him and watched him fearfully as he knelt beside her. Though the panic in her eyes was apparent, the professor did not speak; her need was too urgent. Instead, he wiped the drying blood out of her eyes and worked to loosen the duct tape over her mouth. She fought him at first, but when she saw Willa Banks coming up the trail, she held herself motionless for the professor. Her eyes were locked on Branden, and they spoke terror.

Once Branden had her mouth free of the tape, she asked, "Am I safe now?" in a scarcely audible whisper.

Branden nodded and took a moment to smooth her hair with a gentle palm. He motioned for Banks to work her bindings free as he flipped his cell phone open.

Banks started fumbling at the girl's bindings, muttering, "Mattie, Mattie. What have they done to you?"

Mattie popped her hands free as soon as Banks had her bindings loose. She threw her arms around Banks's neck and clung to her as if Willa were her last hope to live.

Branden punched in Ellie Troyer-Niell's number down at the jail and waited for the call to go through, all the while scanning the area visible to him for signs of Albert Erb. When Ellie picked up, Branden said urgently, "Ellie! Send help! We need an ambulance, Ellie. Behind the Willa Banks property on Nisley Road."

Banks shouted out her address, and Branden asked, "Did you get that?"

In answer to Ellie's questions, the professor said:

"Paramedics, Ellie. And a search team."

"Right. Search dogs, too."

"No, we need the whole crew. Ask Bruce to call in the night shift people."

"A girl, Ellie—Mattie Erb. She's been tied up in the woods."

"She's covered with blood. It's her cousin Albert who's missing. Maybe four years old. Taken off, I don't know. He's not here. Might be dead."

"No, I think someone took him and tied Mattie up."

"No."

"His hair's been cut off."

"Clothes are off, too. No, Ellie. We've trampled the scene already."

"Speed is our ally here."

"No, just send me everything you've got. I'll have Willa Banks out by the road to guide everybody back here."

"What? No, I can't tell. She's conscious. I don't see any cuts or wounds. If all this blood were hers, she'd be dead."

14

Saturday, May 12
11:30 A.M.

MATTIE ERB trembled, with her eyes closed, and buried her bloody forehead against the professor's neck. He held her with both arms and cradled the back of her head with his hand, waiting where he had found her for the paramedics. When he tried to pass her to the first paramedic to arrive, she clung to him as if he were life itself—her last, best hope to breathe. Gently he pulled her arms loose, and she started crying. So Willa Banks took her into her arms again and let the paramedics look the girl over while she held her.

Concerned for the parents, the professor took Mattie back from Willa, and said, "Can you get her parents, Willa?" and Banks started off through the woods, heading toward the back of Enos Erb's house.

While they tended to Mattie, Branden started pacing off wider and wider circles among the trees. Twenty-five yards farther down the trail, he found a shiny mass of bloody entrails heaped on the ground. His stomach lurched, and he cried out.

One of the paramedics came up to him, saw the organs on the ground, and blurted out a curse. "I don't think that's human," he said. "That can't be human. It's a dog or a pig, something like that. It's got to be!"

"OK, look," Branden said. "We've got to hope that this is some animal. That the boy has been kidnapped. If we assume he's dead and he's not, we'll have lost what chance we have to find him."

"Right," the paramedic said and knelt beside the entrails.

Branden ran back down the trail toward Banks's property and met Ricky Niell, who was just coming up to the edge of the trees. They stepped aside to let two more paramedics head up the trail to Mattie.

Off to the side, Branden explained, "I think someone has kidnapped Albert Erb, maybe killed him. He's four. His clothes are back there on that trail. And his hair has been cut off. Something's been gutted. There's blood smeared over Mattie's forehead. Somebody planned this."

Niell asked, "Why in the woods?"

"These two kids have been sneaking into the woods here to play. They're cousins."

"So somebody knew that," Ricky said. "Somebody knew they'd be here."

Branden nodded. "I don't think the families know that they've been coming here. It's got to be a neighbor, maybe a relative. Nuts, Ricky, I can't believe we're thinking like this."

"They're neighbor kids?" Ricky asked.

"Right. Albert goes with the Israel Erbs on the other side of Nisley. Mattie is an Enos Erb kid, from right there on the other side of those trees."

Niell saw two deputies approaching and he called out, "Roadblocks, Pat. A mile in each direction."

Pat Lance turned her partner around, and they ran.

Branden said to Niell, "We're gonna have to search the woods back here."

Niell asked, "How about the homes?"

"Those, too. Israel's, Enos's, and all the neighbors."

"This is going to take too much time," Ricky complained.

"He shaved off Albert's hair, Ricky," Branden said. "And I think he must have brought other clothes for him. This was planned by someone who knew these kids. This guy knew these kids were gonna be right here."

"It could be a she, or a couple," Ricky offered.

"Not as likely. But cutting Albert's hair should mean a disguise, as if he were intending to run with the child. Whoever did this thought it through ahead of time. If he's still alive when we find him, Albert will be disguised."

"Who knew they'd be here?" Ricky asked.

"Willa Banks, for one," Branden said. "She headed off toward Enos Erb's house right after we found Mattie."

"Any Amish who knew they'd be here?"

Branden paused, thought about that, and shook his head. "There are two bishops feuding out here, but I think they've got everybody clamped down pretty tight. They're all going to be accounted for. No Amish would have an opportunity to put this together."

Chief Deputy Dan Wilsher approached the tree line and asked, "Roadblocks, Ricky?"

"Done," Niell said.

"Have we got clothing from the boy?" Wilsher asked Branden.

"Clothing and hair, plus there are animal guts on the ground," Branden answered. "Back on the trail. There's a pair of clippers, too."

Around the corner of Willa Banks's big metal garage, two dog teams arrived with their handlers. Robertson was right behind them. He let the dog teams move through to the trail and then joined Niell, Branden, and Wilsher at the edge of the woods. "Where are the families?" he asked.

"It's the two families on these farms," Branden said. "One right next door and the other across the road. They're all Erbs. I sent Willa Banks to get Enos Erb and his wife."

Robertson flipped his phone open and dialed Ellie. "Dan Wilsher will organize a search," he told her. "Send everybody to Willa Banks's front yard."

Wilsher ran toward the front, clumsy in his black leather loafers, but determined.

"Ricky's gonna handle roadblocks," the sheriff said into the phone. "Send every cruiser, Ellie. We're gonna box this rat in."

He switched off and said, "I want a noose around his neck, Niell. I want you to pull it so tight his eyes will pop."

Ricky ran toward the road.

Robertson asked Branden, "Is there anything I need to see back there?"

"Once they bring Mattie out," Branden said, "it's just forensics. Let the dogs do their jobs."

"Then you and I are on the families," Robertson said.

There was a shout from the trail, and Branden and the sheriff stepped aside to let a paramedic carry Mattie Erb out of the woods. Her eyes were ranging left and right, as wide as saucers. Her forehead and hands had been cleaned up, but traces of blood still showed around her fingernails and eyebrows. In a voice as thin as paper and as tragic as abuse, she said, "I want my mommy."

Robertson stepped forward instinctively, but one of the paramedics said, "We've got this, Sheriff." The man carrying Mattie ran forward with her and laid her down on a gurney that was just being brought around from the front. Then Branden and Robertson fell in behind the paramedics and walked Mattie out to the road.

There was nothing more the two men could do for her. They watched the paramedics search Mattie for wounds and had to stand back to let it happen.

Dan Wilsher was organizing groups of deputies and firefighters on the front lawn of Willa Banks's property. He had laid his suit jacket on the grass, and he was starting to sweat under the arms. Niell would be placing the roadblocks where they'd do the most good. The dogs were already in the woods, working the scent. All of this had been accomplished in less than an hour from the time Ellie had taken the professor's first call. Robertson looked at Branden and asked, "What are we neglecting?"

Before he could answer, there was a crashing of leaves and branches behind the two men, at the tree line dividing the two properties, and when Branden and Robertson turned around, they saw little Enos Erb forcing his way through the tangles under the trees, shouting, "Stop! Stop! They'll be killed!"

Then Enos saw Mattie in the back of the ambulance, and he buckled at the knees and fell over onto his hands with a strangled cry.

Branden ran to him, helped him up from the ground, and said, "Mattie's OK."

But Erb snatched desperately at his sleeve and said, "If you go after Albert, they're gonna kill him."

* * *

Vera Erb ran past Enos and the professor. At the back of the ambulance, she reached out for Mattie and caught her when she leapt into her arms. Branden turned back to the trees and saw all of Mattie's brothers and sisters lined up, in denim vests and cotton dresses, watching silently as Vera kissed her daughter repeatedly, and chastised her, too. The little girl rubbed her fingers on her mother's cheeks, trying to dry the tears, and she spoke Albert's name time and again.

Robertson faced Enos and said, "You'd better explain yourself, sir," and Enos mouthed words helplessly, unable to give voice to his fears.

Branden drew the dwarf aside and said, "You have to tell us, Enos. You have to tell us what you know."

Behind him, a man said, "I can tell you better," and Enos managed a single word, "Israel!"

Israel Erb was as tall as Robertson, easily topping six feet. He was dressed in a black Sunday suit, with gray hair spilling out under his black felt hat. He said to Robertson, "One of the children took our Benny's phone and has been using it. We didn't know she had it. We didn't even know Benny had a phone. But, Benny got a call two hours ago, and the child answered the ring. A man said, 'Stay home. Lock your doors, or you will never see the children again.'"

Branden asked, "That's why you wouldn't come to your door?"

Israel nodded. "I sent one boy on foot to Preacher Hershberger's.

He's closest. We counted one child missing from our household—Albert. The other child, I can see, was Mattie."

A paramedic came up to Robertson and reported, "There's nothing wrong with her, Sheriff. The little girl is fine."

Robertson and Branden stepped aside to let Vera carry Mattie toward home. Enos fell in behind Vera, and the whole family of children followed them back through the narrow stand of trees at the property line.

Robertson said to Israel, "You know that's not good enough. I need to talk to the girl who took that call."

Israel nodded agreement and said, "Our Mary had the phone. We will wait across the road."

"You keep them all right there on the farm, Mr. Erb," Robertson growled. "When I get around to you, I'm going to need some answers."

Branden watched the taller Erb walk back across the road and said, "That's a little harsh, Bruce," to the sheriff.

Robertson complained, "They got that phone call over two hours ago."

Branden said, "Let me talk to Enos. I can do that better than you. And let me question Mattie. You'd just scare her."

Robertson gave a dismissive wave of his hand and fixed his gaze on Dan Wilsher. "I'm going to help Dan," he said and walked off to join his chief deputy.

Branden checked the tree line and saw that the Erbs had all filed home. He started to follow them but heard Willa Banks behind him, saying, "You mark my words, Professor. That rat Miller is up to no good."

When he turned to her, the professor saw Willa Banks standing on the lawn with her fingers wrapped around another can of beer. She had a rusty lawn chair under her arm. Setting her beer on the lawn, she opened the folding chair in front of him and sat down. "Think I'll watch a spell," she pronounced.

"You're not going to . . ."

"Help out? No, Professor. I'm gonna sit here and watch some-one make a fool out of Andy Miller. This is going to boil down to money, and I want to see what that sanctimonious Rat Puke is going to do about it—pardon my French."

15

IT WAS WILLA BANKS who had roused the Enos Erbs from
their home. While Branden held little Mattie in the woods, she circled around and came up behind their house. She ran up to the back
door and proceeded to pound so insistently that Enos had to answer her. This Branden learned from Enos, while they waited in the
front parlor of the dwarf's home for Cal Troyer to arrive. Branden
had called Troyer as soon as Robertson had walked off to join the
search team.

While they waited for Cal, the professor tried a few gentle questions with little Mattie, but she would not speak. Her mother put
her to bed. When Cal was seated, Branden started questioning Enos.

"Was it Bishop Miller who told you about the kids—about the
phone call on Benny's cell? Is that who was in the buggy when I
came out?"

Enos nodded anxiously. Mute, he looked as if he'd never speak
again.

"Enos," Cal said. "You have to talk to us now. Tell us what you
know."

Erb's expression was a mixture of panic and confusion, like a
condemned man asked to choose between poison and the noose.

Branden said, "Mattie is safe, Enos. Now think of Albert."

The house was as quiet as a courtroom waiting to hear a verdict.
Enos lifted his palms helplessly, swallowed a lump, and said, "The
bishop."

"Yes—the bishop?" Cal urged.

"He said we had best all wait in our homes. He told us it was wrong to hate. It was wrong to condemn this man. He told us to pray. But I got so panicked. I got so lost. Oh, I am weak!"

"I don't think you are," Branden said.

Enos gave the impression of a man interrogating himself on the question of integrity. "The bishop said that a strong man would suffer the least right now. That he would hold true. Never hate. Never condemn."

"That's probably true," Cal said. "But this is unusual. Nobody would blame you now."

"We are to pray," Enos said, sounding sure.

"Rightly so," Cal replied.

"We are to trust God to know best," Enos said with greater confidence.

"Even more," Cal said. "Especially now, Enos. But help us. Tell us what you know."

Tears spilled onto his cheeks. "It's so hard."

He pulled out his handkerchief, blew his nose, and wiped his eyes with the back of his hand. He lifted his hip off the chair and stuffed the wadded handkerchief deep into his side pocket.

"Thing is, Cal," he said, "I don't know anything. Only what Willa told me—that they had found Mattie—and only what the bishop said—Albert was missing, too. And that they'd be killed if we tried to find them."

* * *

On the front lawn, Branden and Troyer stood alone, watched by a dozen pairs of eyes from the Enos Erb house. Branden turned his back to the eyes and told the pastor, "That bought the kidnappers time, Cal. The phone call kept these two families locked in their homes instead of out looking for their children. That bought time."

"But why take the children, Mike?" Cal asked.

"Why take the boy and leave the girl behind? And if they—he—needed time, for what?" Branden said.

Cal said, "Maybe two kids were too much for him to handle alone."

"Then why not kill her?"

Cal shrugged his confusion.

Branden offered, "OK. They—he—wants something."

"What?"

"Don't know."

"From whom?"

"From the Erbs—all of them," Branden said. "He wants something from the Erbs."

"What, Mike? What do Amish have? What can Amish give?"

Branden turned to look back at the house full of eyes. He gave it a long time, intending Enos to see his worry. To see his dilemma. If the dwarf hadn't told him everything he knew, he wanted him to realize his error. Turning back to Cal, Branden said, "He knows more than he's told us."

"We should try Israel," Cal said. "He seems to know the most here."

"No, Cal. Not Israel. It's the preacher who knows the most here. While I talk with Israel, you're gonna hunt down Preacher John Hershberger. If he wants to be a bishop so bad, let's offer him a challenge."

16

Saturday, May 12
12:35 P.M.

CAL RETRIEVED his car from the roadblock at the school on Mt. Hope Road and drove east to find Hershberger. Branden crossed Nisley on foot and found Robertson walking down from Willa Banks's place. The sheriff asked Branden, "What'd you get from Erb?"

Branden said, "Benny Erb had a cell phone."

Robertson croaked out, "We know that already!" and rubbed his short gray hair nervously.

The sheriff looked undone by worry. His tie was stuffed into the side pocket of his suit coat, and his collar was loose. His neck was scratched red, and his mouth seemed pulled into an irreversible frown. Shiny beads of perspiration rode the top of his lip, and his eyes were restless, as if he'd missed a dose of his antidepressant. He took his handkerchief out, used it to wipe his lip and then his forehead, and asked, "Where'd Cal go?"

"He's going to find John Hershberger. The preacher. The one who's gonna be bishop of a new congregation."

"Ellie told me this was Andy Miller's district," Robertson said.

"There's a split. Hershberger is taking half the church off on the modern side. Miller asked him to go form a new congregation."

"Over what?" Robertson asked. "No, don't tell me. It's going to be something stupid like radios."

"Science projects at the college."

"Is that going to mix in here with these kids, Mike?"

"I don't know," Branden said. "I really don't know what's going on out here."

"This the same Benny who died out here a couple of weeks ago, the Benny with the phone?"

"Benny Erb. He fell off a ladder in that little store right there. But Enos Erb asked me yesterday to look into that."

"Why?" Robertson asked as he studied the Israel Erb house. He started walking up the drive.

Branden walked along and said, "Benny was a dwarf."

"Couldn't climb a ladder?" Robertson asked.

"Right. You got that fast."

The sheriff mounted the front steps of the house and lifted his hand to knock, but Israel Erb was already at the door, and he pushed out to join the men on the porch. The silence the professor had noted before was still in force. There was no movement or noise inside the house.

Israel said, "Is there news of Albert?"

"No," Robertson answered. "We've expanded the search."

"Do you expect to find him, Sheriff?"

Robertson eyed the man, took his measure, and gently said, "Not right away."

Erb nodded gravely.

Branden said, "Enos told us that it was Hershberger who told him about his Mattie being taken."

Erb said, "Him and Bishop Miller. They went together."

"So Hershberger knew right away," Branden asserted. "He knew they'd been kidnapped."

"I sent a boy to him when we found the phone and learned about the call," Israel said. "Our Mary took the call. We sent for the preacher right then, because he lives close by. He decided to get the bishop."

"OK," Robertson said. "So you waited inside, and so did Enos. What else?"

"You came," Israel replied. "You are here."

Robertson stroked his handkerchief impatiently across his brow and said, "That's all, Mr. Erb? You didn't search? Didn't go looking for them? Why?"

"The caller told Mary that the children would be harmed if we did."

Robertson shook his head with disgust.

Branden said, "Hershberger and Miller just went home after they talked to Enos?"

"I didn't watch to see."

"What in the world were you doing?" Robertson demanded.

"Praying, Sheriff. We were praying."

Robertson started to bark out, "For crying out . . ." and Branden cut him off, asking, "Can we talk to Mary?"

The big sheriff drew his intensity back inside and waited impatiently for an answer.

Israel put his head through the door, and a girl of about fourteen came sheepishly out onto the porch. "Mary, please tell them," Israel said.

Mary Erb searched the faces of the men for some comfort, took a careful breath, and said, "The man said don't come out or we would never see Mattie and Albert again."

Though not a dwarf, Mary was short and would probably not reach average height. Her brown hair was put up in a bun under her prayer cap, and her olive dress ran long, to the tops of her black shoes. Her eyes were brown and restless with anxiety, and she had a dish towel in her fingers, working it like prayer beads.

"He used their names?" Branden asked.

Mary hesitated. "I'm not sure, now."

"What else?" Robertson commanded harshly.

Tears welled in the corners of Mary's eyes, and Branden knelt to face her.

Eyes level with the professor's, Mary said, "We were not to look for them. That's what the man said."

Branden pushed up from his knees and shot Robertson a glance. Then he said to Israel, "We can use the phone, Israel. We can take information from it. That'll tell us who called."

A tragic sorrow bled into Israel's gaze. It was mixed with the long vistas of resignation. With the long memories all Amish carry of the persecutions in Europe. He raised his palms helplessly and said, "We do not have the phone."

The sheriff started to growl out something profane, but Branden turned on him so fast that he choked it back and bit down on his temper as if he'd been slapped in the face.

Carefully, Branden said, "Israel, that's the one thing right now that can lead us to the person who has Albert."

Israel whispered, "We got rid of the phone. Such gadgets have no place here."

Branden asked, "OK, where did Benny get it?"

"I don't know."

"How did you know he had one?"

Israel shrugged.

Mary said, "Benny said he got it from a friend he met. He told us kids that. After Benny died, Daniel got it out of his apartment and gave it to me. He knew I liked it."

Branden turned back to her and leaned over to ask, "Do you know who gave it to Benny, Mary?"

"No," Mary said with a quivering lip.

"Do you know how long he had it before he died?"

"No."

"Did he ever tell you his number?"

"No."

"Did he ever let you use it?"

"No. He said it was for grown-ups."

"You didn't call your friends? You didn't want to use it?"

"No."

Branden pressed, "And Daniel just gave it to you, Mary?"

"He said he didn't like it."

"He's your brother?"

"Yes."

"Did you like it, Mary? Did you like the phone?"

"Yes," Mary said and started to cry. "I just carried it around. Then I got that call."

Branden straightened up. He held Mary's eyes and judged that she was telling the truth. To Israel he said, "Do any of your children —maybe the older ones—maybe Daniel—know what Benny's number was?"

"I don't know," said Israel.

Robertson started to speak again, but again Branden cut him off.

"You see, Mr. Erb," the professor said, "if we had Benny's number, we could trace all of his calls. We could use computers to see who he had been talking to."

Israel hesitated, thought, and said, "If any of them had used the phone, they would have told me."

"You're guessing," Branden prodded. "You're not sure."

More hesitation from Erb. "I believe that they would have told me. They would have told me today, while we were praying."

Frustrated, but unwilling to show it, Branden decided to try shock. "Do you know that Enos thinks Benny was murdered?"

That registered on Israel's face as a clear and cruel surprise. He gasped a quick breath and appeared to wobble on his legs.

Branden said, "Benny wouldn't have fallen off a ladder."

Groaning with his effort, Enos Erb mounted the steps to the porch and said, "He is right, Israel. Benny didn't want you to know, but he couldn't climb ladders anymore."

Deep sorrow filled Israel's countenance. He staggered back a pace and braced himself against the front door. Enos continued forward and said, "Bishop Miller is wrong, Israel. We have to trust the English."

Robertson demanded, "Give us the phone, Mr. Erb."

Shaking his head, Israel moaned, "We don't have it. I don't know where it is."

Heat shot into Robertson's face as if he were biting down on burning flares. He advanced on the taller Erb, and looked ready to strike the man.

But from the lawn below, the men heard, "I burned it, Sheriff. I burned the phone."

When they turned around, they saw Preacher John Hershberger standing next to Cal.

17

Saturday, May 12
12:55 P.M.

ROBERTSON BARKED, "You men all wait here," and pulled Branden down off the porch.

He took the professor down Nisley Road about thirty yards, out of earshot. With his back to the porch, he gesticulated wildly, asking, "Are they watching?"

Branden understood the theater of irascibility that Robertson intended and said, "You've got your audience, Sheriff."

"I swear, Mike, I'm too old for this crap."

"You need to let Cal and me handle the Amish."

"I know. I don't need this kind of aggravation. Just tell them that you talked me out of something threatening."

Branden said, "I'd like to know what Dan and Ricky have got for us before I go back up there."

Robertson took his cell phone out. As he dialed, he watched the porch and saw an animated discussion under way. Good, he thought. Let them sweat a little.

The first call went to Dan Wilsher. Robertson could see his chief deputy some fifty yards down the road when he answered the sheriff's call, so the two men faced each other over the distance and talked. Branden heard Robertson's end of the conversation.

"What have we got, Dan? How many? No, start with the Banks's house and garage. OK, so tie her up if you have to. Right. Right. Then go through these two Erb farms, Dan. The works. Everywhere, Dan. Everywhere big enough for the body of a four-year-old boy. No. No. Yes, get Wayne County down here if you need the help. OK. But Dan—hurry."

He switched off and said, "Dan's search has turned up nothing, Mike, but they're just getting started on houses and buildings. The dogs are two miles away, working on scent."

"Willa Banks won't be a problem," Branden predicted.

Robertson said, "Don't know; don't care. She gets in the way, I'll arrest her."

Next Robertson called Ricky Niell. After a few brief questions, all he had for Branden was a shake of his head, and "Ricky's got nothing."

"We got out here too late," Branden said.

Robertson nodded. "I'm gonna call down to the jail."

Back on his phone, the sheriff said, "Robertson here. OK, Ellie. Right, then you know. I want an Amber Alert for Albert Erb, four years old. What? OK, I'll come in. I'll be right there, Ellie. Twenty minutes. Thirty, tops."

Branden asked, "So, you're going to let us handle Hershberger?"

"I've got no choice, Mike. Ellie needs help, and I'm supposed to sign off on one of these Amber Alerts, anyway. Ricky's watching the roads, and Dan's running the search teams. I'd just be in the way out here."

"As soon as I have something," the professor said, "I'll call you."

Robertson took a grim look back at the Amish men on the porch and said, "We're too late, Mike. They should have called us right away."

18

Saturday, May 12
2:00 P.M.

WITHOUT ROBERTSON, the conversation with John Hershberger was a civil one. More than once, Branden found himself
thankful for that blessing.

Cal sat with Branden, on Israel Erb's front porch, opposite Israel
and Hershberger. They had coffee and sandwiches, and they talked.
Enos stood by Israel's chair and fiddled nervously with the butt of
an old cigar. He never spoke.

At one point, Branden asked, "You're really a Modern, John?"

Hershberger smiled weakly and stroked his chin whiskers. "To a
degree, Professor. Concerning medicine—yes. But, the Good Book
says, 'Be ye separate' from the world."

"What does the Good Book say about telephones?" Branden
asked.

"You know it says nothing," Hershberger replied evenly.

"So, you are to use your judgment," Branden concluded.

"Our discernment, rather," Hershberger corrected.

Going to the heart of the matter, Branden asked, "Anybody's
discernment, John, or just the bishop's? Your discernment, when
you've formed your new modern church?"

"A bishop is called to judge—to discern. We are all made strong
through submission."

"To whom?"

"To God, of course. To the Book."

"And what of modern medicines?"

Here Hershberger stalled. He considered a moment and said, "Our lives are supposed to be hard. Sacrifice and struggle teach us humility. Humility enhances grace. And God is glorified through our sufferings, if we are submissive. But, if God has made medicine possible, then we should accept it. That's where Andy Miller and I differ."

Cal asked, "Needless suffering, John? How is God's Grace amplified by needless suffering?"

"If God has chosen us for trial of our faith—and we are all tried, the Bible promises—then we see that as a blessing. The trial of our faith is a blessing because it produces maturity. Our lives are surrendered to God so that we may know the full stature of a man in Christ-likeness."

"Do you reject phones?" Branden asked.

"Yes."

"Do you reject electricity?" Branden asked, suspecting the answer.

"We do."

"Even batteries?" Branden said.

"Yes."

Standing next to him, Israel cleared his throat, unhappy with Hershberger's answers.

Hershberger corrected himself. "Where a business is required to have light for safety, we allow a bulb. But in Israel's store, there, he has only gas mantles for light. We will not compromise for reasons of convenience. Only for safety, when the law requires. And for medicine."

There it is, Branden thought—the fringe of inconsistency. He knew what further questioning would bring. Whatever compromises the preacher would allow with the world, he'd hold his people steadfastly to submission. To submission to him, once he had formed his church. The people of the church, the *Gemie,* were made perfect and whole only by submission to one another, submission to God, and submission to a single earthly authority—their bishop. And it didn't matter where the line on culture had been drawn. It didn't matter now, and it didn't matter in the sixteenth century when Europe's Anabaptists had been persecuted. They had drawn a line in the cultural sand in order to fit their society into a submissive posture toward God, because they had been powerless, as pacifists, to stop the intense persecution for their beliefs about adult baptism. They had done this according to their best understanding of the scriptures, and now there was to be little compromise with the modern world. In the twenty-first century, they lived on sixteenth-century peasant farms for their faith, and cell phones and electricity had no place in their world. But, ironically, modern medicine did.

Hershberger repeated, "'Be ye separate' from the world, Professor Branden. It is not a request. It is God's command on our lives."

Branden asked, "Aren't surrender and submission nothing more than fatalism?"

"Without faith, yes," Hershberger answered.

Branden followed with, "Isn't faith, in the presence of danger like this, just an excuse, John? Nothing more than an elaborate cop-out?"

Hershberger answered softly, "Not if it is redemptive. Not if it is restorative, Professor. Faith requires greater strength than violence. We are nonresisters to violence because we understand faith."

Branden knew it would be pointless to argue. He cared, really, only about the phone. It was his only link to Albert's kidnappers. "You burned the phone?" he asked. "You actually burned it?"

"In my wood stove, in the kitchen, Professor. I burned it before it could harm us any more. I burned it to ash and molten plastic, and I scattered it all in the fields."

Cal offered, "What if Benny left something behind, John? What if we had his number? Would you let us use computers to find Albert?"

Israel Erb leaned forward on his chair to hear the preacher's answer.

Hershberger said, "We don't expect English to understand obedience."

Heat flushed quickly into Cal's neck, but he calmed himself and asked, "Are Benny's things still in his room? Is it still his room? Can we search it?"

Hershberger looked to Israel for an answer.

Israel said cautiously, watching Hershberger closely, "We had to clean it up after Benny died. He left it a mess, everything thrown around."

Branden stood up.

Cal asked, "May we see it?"

Israel waited for Hershberger to reply.

Hershberger said, "This would not diminish us. This does not mock God. We can submit to this."

19

Saturday, May 12
3:10 P.M.

BENNY ERB had lived in the second apartment attached to the back of the addition on Israel Erb's house. Hershberger and the two Erb men waited outside while Branden and Troyer went inside to search for information about Benny's cell phone.

The single door opened to a combination sitting room–bedroom, with a small bathroom behind a door at the back wall. Light came in from two west-facing windows, but the openings were small, so Israel produced two kerosene lamps and a box of kitchen matches. When Troyer had the lamps burning, he set one on a bedside stand and the other on a small dresser.

Once they had the room well lighted, Branden said, "This Benny had a lot of stuff."

Clothes for a dwarf were jumbled in a pile on the bed, as if Benny had just done laundry and brought the clothes in off the line. Branden searched all the pockets of the clothes.

Cal went through the top two drawers on the dresser and found more clothes. The pockets all proved empty, but in the bottom drawer, Cal found nearly a hundred business cards scattered loosely with some paper money and dozens of coins.

Cal said, "Mike, look at this," and started sorting the business cards from the money.

When they had most of the cards stacked on top of the dresser,

Branden read out the names of the first two dozen or so. There were lawyers, contractors, dentists, doctors, professors, landscapers, carpenters, cab drivers, real estate agents, bankers, insurance agents, and many others in the stack. There appeared to be a card for every type of professional in Holmes County. Branden took up one and said, "Here's Nina Lobrelli's."

In the nightstand, they found old matchbooks from area restaurants. In the bathroom, they found courtesy soaps from ten different motels. Under his bed, there were bumper stickers and flyers from a score of political candidates. In the trunk at the end of his bed, Benny had a collection of box tops from carryout and delivery pizza places, all cut to the shape of a circle so they would stack together in the trunk. Under one window, a small set of shelves held free cookbooks from the Holmes County fair, hand tracts from churches and revivals, magazines from doctors' offices, pamphlets about kites and radio-controlled airplanes, an English-German dictionary, and a stack of old raffle tickets bound together with a red rubber band.

Nowhere in the apartment was there evidence of Benny's phone. There were no phone numbers scribbled on scraps of paper. There were no phone company bills and no cell phone accessories. There were no address books with phone numbers.

Branden and Troyer carried the lamps outside and asked the Erbs if Benny had any other places where he kept things. They asked if Benny had an account at a bank. Did he see a doctor, dentist, anyone like that? Had he used the services of a lawyer? Did he ride in taxis, busses, or the vans that went to Wal-Mart? Did Benny correspond with anyone regularly through the mails? Had he ever posted announcements or letters in the *Sugarcreek Budget* newspaper? The answers they got were either "No" or "We don't know."

Thus there was no way to trace his calls. There was no evidence that he had ever made any calls. If he had talked on a phone to anyone, Branden and Troyer would never know it. And if they used the cards, papers, magazines, and other contents of his apartment to track down the people the little man had known, they'd be at it for over a year.

* * *

"We struck out," Branden said to Robertson on his phone. "There's not going to be a phone number to trace."

He was standing on the pavement of Nisley Road, at one of Ricky Niell's roadblocks. Two Wayne County deputies had searched his truck. They seemed bored and tired, and withdrew when Branden made his call.

Robertson asked, "You gonna stay out there, Mike?"

"No, I'm driving back."

"We're searching the whole township, but I think this kid is gone."

Branden considered that and said, "If this is a pedophile, he's not going to contact the family again."

"I know," Robertson said.

"There's the Amber Alert, still," Branden said.

"There is that," Robertson agreed.

"This isn't going to end well, Bruce."

"I know. Look, Mike, Missy is finished with Cathy Billett's body. She says there's no sign of a struggle. No bruising, nothing like that. She tested under Cathy's fingernails, but it's not conclusive, since Eddie admitted she scratched him a lot. You know—an aggressive lover."

"So, it was suicide," Branden said.

"Missy says there's no way to tell. She says there's nothing to suggest Cathy Billett didn't throw herself off that bell tower, but that doesn't prove she did."

"Her parents were supposed to fly in today," Branden said.

"They're already here. Arne Laughton brought them down to Missy at the hospital. She says she's going to release the body after her toxicology samples come back from the BCI labs."

"What about Eddie?" Branden asked.

"Saw him, Mike, and sent him home already."

"You were going to interview him again."

"Yeah, I did that. We just finished."

Branden waited.

Robertson said, "Mike, he's too stupid for words. I'm surprised you guys are handing him a degree."

"That's not the Eddie I know," Branden said.

"Then he's been rendered stupid by grief, Mike."

"Eddie's not stupid, Bruce, even if he is stricken with grief. It's more likely you two didn't exactly 'hit it off' very well. You've had him pegged wrong from the start."

"I don't like rich college kids, Mike."

"I know that, Sheriff. That's what I'm saying."

"OK, so I talked to him," Robertson said. "Point is, he can't have killed Cathy Billett. Not the way I see it. If they had a struggle and she fell, or something like that, then he'd have told us that. The guy's just not smart enough to make something up. And if she fell in a struggle, we would not be charging him with murder, anyway. So it's a wash on my end. We're done."

"OK, look, I'm going home," Branden said. "Call me there."

"You'd have more fun down here at the courthouse, Professor."

"Why's that?"

"Your friend Aidan Newhouse has a crowd of hippie students down here. He's got a little protest march going on."

"He still in those handcuffs?"

"What do you think, Professor?"

20

Saturday, May 12
7:30 P.M.

AFTER SUPPER, the professor finished telling Caroline what he knew, while stretched out on the bed in their second-floor bedroom. Caroline sat in her rose nightgown, brushing her long auburn hair in front of her vanity.

"We're sure he had a phone," Branden was saying, "but Hershberger claims he burned it."

"You don't know the number?" she asked.

"No."

"So that's a dead end."

"Right."

"This Benny sounds like he was a people person, Michael. He had friends all over the county."

"Enos called him a chatterbox."

"We would have liked him, Michael."

Branden nodded his silent agreement and sank deeper into the pillows, hands clasped behind his head. When Caroline had finished brushing her hair, she turned from her mirror and said, "I don't like Aidan Newhouse."

"Where'd that come from?"

"I just don't like him, Michael. He's arrogant. He always has been."

"He's harmless, Caroline."

"No, Michael, he teaches. That's not harmless."

"You don't like him because he's political, Caroline."

"I don't know why you defend him," she replied.

"Aidan and I have been colleagues too long for me to take a dislike to him just because he's theatrical."

"Is that what you call it, Michael? Theatrical?"

"He's theatrical and political. The two go together in his world."

"If you say so."

"Look, Caroline. I got to know Aidan when his son was a student here. He's not a bad character."

"You admit he's a character?"

"But not a bad one."

The doorbell rang and Branden checked his watch. "A late caller?" he said and went downstairs to answer the door.

It was Deputy Pat Lance, in uniform. She was a short, round woman with Germanic features—blond hair, stern blue eyes, and thin lips. Branden invited her in and showed her into the living room. She saw the stack of blue books on the coffee table and said, "I remember those from college."

Branden explained, "I haven't finished my grading."

Lance said, "The seniors are going to graduate Monday," with a slight undertone of interrogation.

Branden laughed. "These are juniors and sophomores. The senior exams are done."

Officiously, Lance nodded her approval and took a seat on the sofa, saying, "Anyway, Dan Wilsher wants me to give you a report."

Caroline came down the stairs in jeans and a Duke University sweatshirt. Lance stood to introduce herself formally, and Caroline said, "Congratulations on joining the sheriff's department."

Caroline sat next to Lance on the couch. The deputy explained, more formally than was necessary, "I've got a report from Dan Wilsher. He has suspended the search for Albert Erb. The search teams are exhausted, especially the dogs. Dan said to tell you, Professor," here she consulted her notes, "'he'd get back out there, tomorrow.'"

Branden waited for her to finish studying her notes and said, "That trail was fresh. I thought the dogs would find something."

"They did," Lance said. "They found the carcass of a small beagle puppy, beside a road about three miles east of the farms. The dog had been gutted. That's what you found on the trail near Mattie—dog's intestines. He used the murder of a puppy to terrorize the children."

Branden shook his head and said, "This was planned." He felt himself drifting into despondency, and muttered, "It's a pedophile."

"Michael!" Caroline objected.

"I think you're right, Professor," Lance said with intensity. "But he made a mistake."

Branden nodded, "He left Mattie behind."

Lance agreed, "The little Amish girl is going to be able to identify him."

"If we ever find him," Branden said. "My guess is he's a thousand miles away by now."

Caroline said, "This isn't like you, Michael. This resignation is not like you at all."

Lance rose and said, "I should be going."

After he had seen Lance to the door, Branden sat back down next to Caroline in the living room and said, "Too many things have happened."

Caroline said, "I know you've been despondent lately, Michael, but you shouldn't give up like this. Dan said he'd have his people out looking again tomorrow."

Several minutes passed as Professor Branden's gaze focused inward. He remembered the visit from Enos Erb in his office. Then, Cathy Billett and Eddie. He remembered Nina Lobrelli's account of her research. Then the strange stillness at the Erb farms. The boy's hair, shorn. The look of stricken resignation in Mary Erb's eyes. Last, he thought of Cal and marveled at the disorganized wanderings of his mind.

Eventually he said, "Cal won't talk to me about his letter."

"You've been grumpy, Michael."

After a pause, Branden said. "I don't want to grade papers anymore."

"What'll you do if you don't teach?"

"I don't mind teaching," the professor said. "What I don't want to do is any more grading."

"Then you've just had a bad couple of days."

"It's more than that, Caroline. I'm tired of the college."

"See how you feel this summer," Caroline said. "You always look forward to fall semester."

"Hmmpf."

"Think about this, Michael. You've just had two rotten days. That's likely all this is."

"Oh, you think so?"

"I do," Caroline said. "Little Benny Erb was murdered. Enos Erb came to see you, but ran off because Cathy Billett threw herself off the bell tower. Bruce was all over Eddie Hunt-Myers's case, and Aidan Newhouse is running around campus like the jerk he is, in handcuffs, of all things. Then, Ben Capper, who's a decent enough fellow, is mixed in with Newhouse, and he'll probably lose his job over cuffing him. Mattie and Albert Erb were kidnapped, and Albert's still missing. This Willa Banks is making a spectator sport out of baiting Andy Miller, and Hershberger burned the only link you had to Benny's phone pal. Arne Laughton has mishandled the Billetts, Cal's not talking about his letter, and you've got thirty blue books to grade before commencement."

The professor looked at Caroline as if to say, "What's your point?" and Caroline said, "You've been depressed right before commencement for the last several years, anyway, Michael. You just don't like saying good-bye to your students, but on top of that, this whole Erb case is starting to slip away from you."

"Is that all?" Branden asked, smiling.

"It's the children who've gotten the worst of this," Caroline said. "Mattie and Albert. If this weren't a case about little children, you'd be more hopeful."

Branden leaned back and stretched out. He closed his eyes, and Caroline drew closer. She brushed her fingers through his hair and said, "We'd fight for our kids, Michael. We'd die before we let someone hurt them."

Eyes closed, Branden said, "We're not pacifists. The Amish are. It's not their way to strike back."

"They could at least defend themselves against evil things," Caroline said. "I'd respect it more if they did that much. At least fight for their children."

"They'll never add violence to violence," the professor said. "They'd rather die."

"What would you fight for, Michael?"

"You. Me. Friends."

"Strangers?"

"Maybe."

"Our kids, Michael, if we had any?"

"With my life. You know that, Caroline."

"Times being what they are, Michael, it may come to that."

"You're worried about terrorists, again," the professor said. "There's likely more danger from a break-in robbery than there is from a terrorist group."

"But we've trained for that, Michael."

"Yes, we have. We're ready. We've thought this through."

"Because if you can't shoot back . . . ," Caroline started.

"You're just a target," the professor finished.

21

CAL SHOWED up at the Brandens Sunday afternoon looking apprehensive, and Caroline drew him into the house and out onto the back porch before he could turn around. There she planted him in a deep wicker chair and said, "Michael needs to speak with you, Cal. You're worrying him."

Cal surrendered to her, palms up, and said, "I'm not going anywhere."

When Caroline had her husband seated next to him, Cal said to them both, "I'm sorry I was cross."

Branden dismissed this with a wave of his hand, but Caroline had the insight to say, "It's OK, Cal. Don't worry."

"It was just so much out of the blue," Cal said. "That letter from Rachel Ramsayer came right out of the blue."

Branden asked, "You getting over it? Made a decision?"

Cal smiled and lifted a plastic medical vial out of his shirt pocket. Then he fished a sterile paper packet out of his pants pocket and opened it to reveal a swab on the end of a plastic stick. He said, "You're supposed to run this swab around inside your cheek, and seal it in this vial."

Caroline and the professor stared back at Cal as if he'd been speaking Amish dialect.

"It's the DNA test to see if Rachel Ramsayer is my daughter."

"Good, Cal," Caroline said. "This is the right decision."

"I didn't want to do this alone," Cal said. "In fact, Caroline, I'd like you to do it for me."

Branden smiled in relief. This was the Cal he knew.

Caroline took the vial from the pastor and reached out for the swab. He opened his mouth, and she ran the swab against the inside of his cheek. When she pushed the swab into the vial, Cal said, "Wish me luck."

22

Sunday, May 13
4:50 P.M.

THE BRANDENS spent the rest of the afternoon at home, Caroline reading in the living room, the professor making calls on his cell phone, out on the back porch. Twice he called Chief Deputy Dan Wilsher and learned only "We're still looking for him, Mike."

Twice he called Ricky Niell, who said each time that the search dogs had been all over the countryside at Calmoutier, and the only scent they could track led to the spot beside the road where they had found the gutted beagle puppy. It was Ricky's best guess that little Albert Erb and his abductor had gotten into a vehicle and driven off. The trail was cold.

When the professor called Bruce Robertson, the sheriff reported that the Amber alert had produced no leads. There hadn't been a single clue to give them hope for the boy.

As he was hanging up with the sheriff, the doorbell rang, and the professor walked through the family room and into the hallway in time to see Caroline letting Eddie Hunt-Myers in at the front door. Eddie had a note-sized envelope, and he pulled out a card, asking if the professor would read it and help him improve it. Caroline left them there and went back to the kitchen.

Branden led Eddie to the couch in the living room and sat in his swivel rocker to read Eddie's note to the Billetts.

Dear Mr. and Mrs. Billett,

I can't tell you how sorry I am about Cathy. She was a wonderful girl and didn't deserve to die like that. I know it was my fault. Please forgive me.

Sincerely yours,

Edwin Hunt-Myers III

P.S. I wish you had liked me more. Maybe this wouldn't have happened.

Branden flinched at the postscript and looked up at Eddie, astonished. "You can't write this, Eddie," he said. "You can't give it to them like this."

"Why not, Professor?" Eddie asked, coming forward on his seat.

"Eddie," Branden said, shaking his head. "This postscript makes it seem as if you think they're to blame, because they didn't like you."

Eddie gave him a blank stare. He didn't get it at all.

Branden tried again. "Eddie, you should just write that you are sorry and leave it at that."

"I thought I had done that," Eddie said.

"You did," Branden sighed. "But the postscript says that you think this wouldn't have happened if they had only liked you more."

"Well," Eddie said slowly, "I do kinda think that."

Branden shook his head again. "You can't write this to the Billetts. They just lost their daughter."

Eddie lowered his eyes and thought. When he looked back to Branden, he seemed dismayed. With shame, he said, "I'm such a screw-up, Dr. Branden. I'm just as stupid as they come."

Branden said, "I'm sure you mean well, Eddie. You should write your note again, but leave off this postscript."

Eddie hung his head sadly. "I should just go somewhere by myself. I just screw everything up for people."

"Eddie," Branden said, "the note is fine without the postscript."

"OK," Eddie whispered. "I'll write it again."

Caroline came into the living room with a tray with three water glasses, but Eddie stood up abruptly and said, "I can't stay, Mrs. Branden."

Caroline said, "I'm sorry to hear that, Eddie," and set the tray on the coffee table.

At the door, Eddie said, "Thanks, Dr. Branden. I would have screwed this up, too."

23

Monday, May 14
MORNING

FOR THE first time at Millersburg College, on the request of the Board of Trustees, the commencement bulletin gave the title of each senior's thesis, with the adviser's name beside it. Branden sat in the oak grove and watched the seniors walk across the stage, and as each one shook the president's hand, Branden read the thesis title. It passed the time for him, and he found that he liked the personal touch it gave. The ceremony began with a prayer for Cathy Billett, and several students came forward to speak of their friendship with her.

The weather that day was unusually warm for northern Ohio, and many of the students and some of the faculty opened their academic gowns to the breeze and sat with their shoes off, toes in the cool grass, according to the Millersburg College tradition. On the back of the commencement bulletin, a note explained that this was done in honor of beloved Professor Newton White, who had died on a hot day in 1922 during commencement, with his shoes off and his robe open to the breeze.

Aidan Newhouse stood during the awarding of degrees, fist raised high overhead, with Ben Capper's manacles shining brightly in the sun. It was his badge of honor, and he wore it well, for a while. By the time the president had worked through the alphabet to the Cs, Aidan's arm had slumped a bit. During the Ds, he found it necessary to move it in a slow circle over his head in order to maintain circulation. In the Hs, Newhouse let his arm drop so he could hold his elbow up with his other hand. In the Qs, the psychology professor sat down, but found new strength in his arm. In the middle of the Ts, he settled for lifting his fist at intervals, when inspiration overcame his fatigue. And during the benediction, he had nothing left. He just sat in his chair with his head bowed for reasons that had nothing to do with the prayer.

Through it all, Branden sat next to him. They had always marched together, lately near the head of the line, having come to Millersburg College the same year. Their seniority surpassed that of all but two active professors ahead of them, plus a half dozen Emeriti who still needed the grand march to give meaning to their lives.

While Newhouse maintained his vigil, Branden watched the students accept their diplomas, mentally noting each one he had taught. Still, because the procession was slow, he had time to study the crowd of parents and relatives who looked on. And once, for about twenty minutes, he observed Chief of Security Ben Capper, who usually organized and directed his security detail on the far perimeter of the assembly. But today Branden observed Capper eyeing Newhouse with disgust, and Branden noticed that when Capper came into view, Aidan Newhouse found new life for his arm.

After the commencement ceremony, the oak grove turned to mild pandemonium as friends in the graduating class sought each other to hug, take pictures, and say their good-byes. Branden stood to the side and let students find him if they wished, and he said his good-byes, too.

Late in the morning, he observed Ben Capper walking briskly out of the oak grove toward his office. Catching sight of Bruce Robertson standing with a distraught couple at the spot below the bell tower where Cathy Billett had died, the professor surmised they were the Billetts from Montana. During it all, President Arne Laughton walked from family to family and stood proudly for photographs when asked. Eddie Hunt-Myers ushered his parents to

Laughton, and the president lingered with them, speaking in hushed voices, no doubt about the Billetts, Branden thought.

Professor Nina Lobrelli sought out Branden and asked about the Amish boy who had been abducted. Branden explained that too much time had passed to contemplate hope for the lad.

Near the end of the morning, as Branden was thinking of walking home, a young woman in a cap and gown approached rather diffidently from the side and stood with him, watching the people mingle. He had never taught her in class, and he was embarrassed not to know her name. Without looking at him, she began to speak softly, and by the time his attention caught up to her words, she was saying, "That was all before he hooked up with Cathy Billett."

Branden turned to her and saw an extraordinarily petite woman with sorrowful eyes. She was no more than five feet tall, and holding a brick in each hand, she might barely have tipped the scales over a hundred pounds. She had short black hair and brown eyes that turned to look at him directly only once. Her complexion was the pale color of coconut, and the muscles in her jaw line were knotting as she spoke.

"Cathy Billett was my best friend," she said, "until they hooked up. After she'd been out with him for the second time, she stopped talking to me. Best friends, Professor, for three years, and she stopped talking to me after two dates with Eddie. That's gotta be a record."

Branden said, "I remember seeing you when Cathy died. You're the girl who tried to slap Sergeant Niell."

"I was trying to get to Eddie," she said with a chilled laugh.

Branden felt a ripple along his spine, an uneasy tension, born of strange insight.

"I don't know your name," Branden said. "I'm sorry."

"Hope Elliot, Professor. Psychology. I did my senior thesis with Professor Wells. I was Eddie's girlfriend, until he dumped me for Cathy."

"I see that Eddie wrote for Newhouse," Branden said, tapping the bulletin and struggling to focus his mind. "Psychology, too."

"He killed her, Professor Branden."

"That's a serious allegation!" Branden exclaimed.

"I know he did it, but nobody can prove it. So he'll probably get away with it."

"Eddie says she jumped," the professor said, adjusting his posture to relieve the tension in his back. "He says he broke up with her, and she jumped."

"Either way, Professor, he killed her. He killed her by how he treated her."

Branden turned to face her fully, and Hope Elliot couldn't look at him. Eyes forward, she said, "It won't be good for me if he sees us talking too much."

* * *

When Hope Elliot walked out of the oak grove, she was crying. She was also watched, Branden noticed, by Eddie Hunt-Myers.

Branden watched Eddie's eyes track Hope to the street, and then he saw them swing back to rest on him. Branden held to his spot, and Eddie pulled his mother over to him. He offered Branden his hand and shook it with abundant goodwill, smiling as if it were the happiest day of his life. Then Eddie introduced his mother. His father joined them, and Eddie introduced him, too. The Hunt-Myerses asked for a picture, and Eddie clamped his arm around Branden's shoulder and smiled for the shot. Eddie's father shook Branden's hand again, and Eddie gave his mother a bear hug. When he released her, there was a light in Eddie's eyes that could have been pride, if it weren't so tinged with sorrow and conflict.

* * *

As the Hunt-Myers family moved off with their graduate, Branden caught a glimpse of Bruce Robertson talking on his cell phone.

Robertson spoke, listened, spoke again with heat, and started across the oak grove toward the professor at a run. Thirty yards out, the sheriff shouted, "Mike! Mike!" as loud as cannon shots, and everybody in the oak grove turned to look.

"We got him!" Robertson shouted. "We got him, Mike! Albert Erb! He's safe. He just walked home on his own."

24

Monday, May 14
2:30 P.M.

"HAS HE said anything at all?" Robertson asked. He was standing on the front porch, talking through the screened door to Israel Erb. The sheriff could see Albert behind Israel, cradled in his mother's arms, head shaved and scalp as white as cotton, in a fresh suit of blue Amish denim.

Israel said, "No, Sheriff. He won't talk. We've tried."

Branden stepped out from behind Robertson and asked Israel, "Do you still have the clothes he was wearing?"

On the steps behind Branden stood Dan Wilsher in a blue suit, his gray hair lifting in the breeze. Behind him Ricky Niell, in uniform, was clicking his gold pen nervously. Cal Troyer waited on the lawn below, and beside him were Missy Taggert with her medical bag and Willa Banks with her endless curiosity. Branden's white truck was parked in the drive, in front of two cruisers and the coroner's wagon. Missy had already explained to Robertson her need to examine the boy. Cal had objected, fearing Albert was already too traumatized. They had agreed that she should start with the English clothes Albert had worn home, and examine him only if it proved to be wise to do so.

Israel looked the whole scene over anxiously from his side of the screen and said, "Yes. We have the English clothes."

He turned back to the room behind him and spoke to an older son in dialect, calling him Daniel. The boy came forward with a plastic Wal-Mart bag bulging with clothes and a pair of pink flip-flops. Israel held the door open, and Daniel stepped out onto the porch with the bag of clothes. Robertson motioned him down the steps, and Missy Taggert came forward to take the clothes and flip-flops. The boy went back inside.

Next, Robertson said, "We want to talk with him, Mr. Erb. Let us talk to Albert."

Israel stepped to the side, and his wife Hannah carried Albert forward to the screen. Robertson pulled the screened door open, and Albert cringed deeper into his mother's grasp, squirming and whimpering. Hannah had difficulty managing him, so Israel took him from her. He laid Albert prone against his chest and let the boy rest his chin on his father's shoulder. Albert was not facing Robertson, so the sheriff said, "Can you please bring him out here?"

Israel nodded for Hannah to precede him, and he followed with Albert. Robertson got them seated on the front porch and signaled for Cal Troyer to join them. Then Robertson and Branden stepped back. Cal waved them back farther, and the two descended the porch steps.

A warm, soft breeze suggested safety, peacefulness. The rhythmic clanking of the windmill pump bracket kept a slow, regular pace. Troyer could hear the beat of the windmill and feel the pulse of the breeze, but he dismissed these distracting sensations because of the insistent cry of Albert's shaved head, the damage to the boy as disturbing as a knife wound to his psyche. Miraculously, the lad had made it home on his own. Perhaps that was all Troyer could ask for.

Troyer wanted to lay a hand against the boy's scalp. He wanted to communicate safety and compassion through his touch. He wanted to hold the child. To console him with human tenderness. He searched himself for all of his healing instincts, but he had only his voice—and then only if he chose his words well. He would get one chance at this, and he'd better get it right.

Softly he said, "Hi, little fella. Hi, Albert. My name is Cal. You are safe now, Albert." And Israel translated it into Dietsche.

Nothing but a bit of squirming came from Albert. He wasn't facing Cal and wouldn't turn around.

Cal continued after a pause. "Mattie is safe, too, Albert. I saw her today. She is safe at home." Israel translated.

Cal said more. "The man was scary. I know that, Albert." Israel translated for the boy.

Nobody made a sound. Albert gave no sign that he had heard. Cal kept his sight on the back of the boy's shaved head, and he prayed as he talked.

"I'd like to see your eyes, Albert," Cal said. "You don't have to talk. You can just show me your eyes."

Slowly, Albert lifted his head from his father's shoulder. Branden, Robertson, Wilsher, and Niell kept a silent vigil on the lawn. Hannah Erb had started to cry. Willa Banks stood with her fingers laid against her mouth, scarcely breathing.

Slowly, as slowly as a child can manage, Albert brought himself around so that Cal could see his eyes. Cal was on his knees, his head slightly lower than Albert's. He held his hands softly in front of himself, as if praying, showing Albert that there was no longer any danger. But, when he saw the boy's face, Cal hungered more than prayer to hold the child and weep.

Tears had made Albert's cheeks wet and shiny. His little lip quivered. There was pain there and also fear. Cal could see that plainly. But as for his eyes, Albert held them closed—closed as tightly as he could squeeze them. All the horror was locked inside. He couldn't show his eyes. He would not let the pastor see them.

And understanding what that meant nearly broke Cal Troyer in half.

* * *

Troyer pushed up from his knees with a weariness so heavy that he faltered. He rose up, turned around as Israel carried Albert back into the house, and saw Bishop Andy Miller coming slowly up the steps. Cal stood speechless before the bishop, and Miller laid a gentle hand on the pastor's shoulder. He drew Cal toward the steps and walked down to the lawn with him.

Robertson said, "Cal, I've never seen anything like that."

Andy Miller said, "We need to handle this our way, Sheriff. You need to let us minister to the boy."

"We can take him to a doctor," Robertson argued. "We can help here."

"No," said Miller. "Our ways are best. We know suffering. Our lives are supposed to be hard."

Robertson said, "No offense, Mr. Miller, but that boy needs professional care. At the very least, he needs to be seen by a psychiatrist. He'll need medical attention."

Cal stood listening with his eyes cast to the ground. He heard Missy's wagon start up and drive off.

Miller turned to him and said, "Do you know your Jonah, Pastor?"

Cal nodded his understanding, but he could not look up.

"Jonah 2:8," Miller said. "'All your medicines are worthless idols to me.'"

Cal nodded, and Miller climbed the steps and went inside.

Robertson started after him, but Cal caught his sleeve and held him back with force.

Ricky Niell took a defensive step toward the sheriff, but Robertson raised a palm, saying, "No, Ricky. It's all right."

Cal let go of the sheriff's sleeve and said, "There are no answers here for us, Sheriff. If he ever starts talking again, he won't tell us any more than he already has."

"What's that?" Willa Banks asked from the side. "What has he told us?"

Troyer turned to her and said, "That it's too terrible for a little boy's eyes. That it's too terrible for words."

* * *

Willa Banks walked home alone to her trailer and shut herself inside. Robertson took Chief Deputy Dan Wilsher back toward

Millersburg, saying, "I'm going back to see what Missy can find on the clothes."

Ricky Niell followed in the second cruiser, leaving Branden and Troyer standing on the drive, next to the professor's truck. Branden studied the closed front door of the house and said, "This can't be his plan."

Cal asked, "What?" consumed by sorrow.

"This can't be his plan—the creep who took these kids, Cal. This can't be his plan."

Bitterly, Cal growled, "He's already gotten away with it, Mike."

"How do you figure that?" Branden asked.

"If the kids can't describe him or can't pick him out of a line-up, we'll never get him. All he has to do is go away and stay away."

"If you're right," Branden said, "then he's already gotten what he wants out of them."

"What's that?" Cal asked.

"Don't know."

"It makes no sense," Cal said. "He should have killed them. Most of these creeps would have killed them."

"So," Branden said, "he got what he wants, and he knows they're so young and scared that they'll never be able to help us catch him."

"If you're right and he has what he wants," Cal said, "then what is that?"

Branden did not answer the question. He had nothing to offer. He looked back at the house, closed to the world of the English. "Jonah 2:8. What's that, Cal?" he asked at last.

Cal recited, "*Those who cling to worthless idols forfeit the grace that could have been theirs.*"

"What does that mean, Cal? Medicines are worthless?"

"No, Mike. He means that they have the grace to endure this without us. He means that they are made whole by their trials—so that grace may increase. He means that they're not going to ask for our help. He considers our medicines to be worthless idols. For his purposes, here, they probably are."

25

Monday, May 14
4:45 P.M.

CAL WAS in no condition to handle the stark reality of the coroner's labs, so Branden dropped him off at his church and drove back north to the hospital alone. As he entered the bright hallway outside Missy Taggert's labs, he heard Taggert arguing with her husband about Albert Erb.

"Knock it off, Bruce," she said, heat flaring in her tone. "I'd no more go back there now than jump out of an airplane."

Branden pushed in through the door to the labs and found the sheriff standing in a far corner, by one of Missy's stainless steel sinks. Missy had her palms planted on a metal examination table, elbows locked, and she wasn't finished. As Branden came in, she added, "If I did go back to look him over, it'd cause him more harm right now than it's worth," and she eyed Branden as if to say, "You try talking to him!"

Branden understood the pressure Missy would put on herself now. To the sheriff he said, "You found a gutted beagle beside the road?"

"Yes," Robertson said. "My people did, anyway."

"So, that's where he left his car when he went after the kids. That's planning, Bruce. That's a level of planning that's pretty sophisticated."

Robertson shook his head. "There's got to be something, Missy. You've got to be able to find something on those clothes."

"I know," Missy said grimly. "It's on me, now. If he gets away with this, it's all on me."

She lifted the Wal-Mart bag from the floor and pulled the items out one at a time. Starting with the larger items, she arranged first a pair of red cotton sweatpants, and then a Spiderman T-shirt, a pair of Jockey briefs in size 3T, and the pink flip-flops. She pulled her illuminated magnifying ring down from the ceiling and bent over to study the sweatpants.

"You boys clear out," she said dismissively. "I'll call you if I find anything."

Robertson moved toward the door, but Branden stayed to ask, "Do you remember the Benny Erb case, Missy? The dwarf from the store in front of Israel Erb's house?"

Distracted, Missy said, "Yes," and moved the magnifying ring over to the Spiderman T-shirt.

Branden said, "That may not have been an accident."

That took several seconds to register with her, but Missy looked up and asked, "What? Benny Erb, right?"

"You ruled that death accidental," Branden said.

"And?"

"His brother says he couldn't climb ladders anymore."

Taggert's eyes narrowed. "He had a broken neck, Mike. He pulled oatmeal off a high shelf, and he was covered in it. Off the top shelf, Mike. He would have needed the ladder to do that. Anybody would."

Branden shrugged. "His brother says he couldn't have done that."

"Legs were stiff, short, like that?" Missy asked.

"Right."

"It was little Albert who found him, Mike—one morning a couple of weeks ago. I examined the body myself. Benny Erb must have been up on that ladder. He hit his head, and his neck was broken."

Branden said, "OK, you were there, and I wasn't. But, still, Missy."

Missy pushed back from her table shaking her head and said, "I don't like this. I don't like making mistakes."

Branden said, "OK, maybe I'm wrong."

"I wouldn't be able to tell, one way or the other, Mike, unless there had been unusual bruising, something like that. Something to suggest force."

26

Monday, May 14
7:15 P.M.

PROFESSOR BRANDEN couldn't shake the image in his mind. It was as if his lids were clicking camera shutters, his brain was film, and the print in his mind would not dissolve—Albert squeezing his eyes shut, tears running freely. After supper, Branden drove Caroline's Miata out to the Nisley Road farms, with Caroline riding in the passenger's seat. He wasn't entirely sure why he was going there, and he wasn't sure why he wanted his wife to go along.

When he turned into the Enos Erb driveway, they saw what looked like all of Enos Erb's children out on the lawn, Mattie excepted. As soon as he pulled in, the two smallest children, maybe six and seven years old, got out of their sandbox and ran inside. Two slightly older girls stood by the swing set and watched the little sports car approach on the gravel drive. Their faces were as blank as the dead, but their eyes stayed fixed on the Brandens. They watched the English strangers roll toward them, then turned in eerie unison to hurry inside.

Two boys of grade school age stopped their game of volleyball. The older of the two put the ball on the ground and motioned for the younger to step under the net. Close together, they watched the car approach. Behind the house the Brandens could hear the drone of a gasoline lawn mower.

A girl of about fourteen years had been hanging clothes on a line beside the swing set, but when she saw the Brandens, she dropped her clothespins into her basket, left it on the grass, and went directly inside.

A lad of about eighteen came out onto the front porch and stood his ground, watching solemnly from above. When he whistled and waved, the two volleyball players walked into the house, never once taking their eyes off the two English in the car.

Behind his son on the porch, Enos emerged and came down the front steps, halfway to the lawn. There he stopped. He was in work clothes—dirty denim trousers, a dark blue shirt, a black hook-and-eyes vest, a summer hat of cream-colored straw, and black leather work boots. A cigar creased his lips, and his eyes held a chill aloofness. He spoke quietly to his boy, and the lad went inside.

On the lawn lay the evidence of a family that had been trying to win back the normal. The volleyball, swing set, and clothes were now abandoned. The gas mower behind the house shut off, and that person no doubt went inside, too.

In the dwarf's expression, Branden could read the timeless suspicion that all back-roads Amish harbor for the modern. He also saw assuredness there—a self-confidence that stemmed from a secure place in the world. A peacefulness that stemmed from faith. This was not the same Enos Erb who had come to his office at the college last Friday morning.

Enos stood on the front steps of his house as a sentinel, having pulled all his people inside before barring the gates of the castle. Branden asked Caroline to wait in the car, and he stepped up to Enos, eye to eye. "I think you're right about Benny, Enos," he said.

Enos shrugged indifference and said, "No matter. It shouldn't trouble you now."

"I just came out to tell you that I'll find the man who did it. And the man who took the kids. I will, Enos, I promise."

"No matter, Professor. You are very kind, but the harm is done."

"Has Mattie started talking, Enos?"

A silent "no" from Erb.

"I don't blame you for being bitter, Enos. Nobody would."

Erb chewed his cigar pensively. "How could bitterness heal the girl, Professor?"

"You're not bitter?"

Enos offered a pensive smile. "I am not permitted bitterness, Professor. That would harm the child more than she has already been harmed."

Branden looked around the abandoned yard. "Have you gone with the Antis, now, Enos? Is that it? Is that what's happened?"

Gravely, Enos said, "There are no Antis anymore."

"What?"

"John Hershberger has confessed his sins to the bishop. The bishop has asked him to keep his people in the church."

"Confessed his sins, Enos? What does that mean?"

"That's between Hershberger and the bishop. We will all hear his confession Sunday, at services. He will be restored."

"Enos, I don't understand what you're telling me."

"Humility is the most beautiful virtue, Professor."

"And Hershberger, Enos, what of him?"

"He seeks humility again," Enos smiled.

"What has he done?"

"It doesn't matter, Professor. The children are safe."

"But they're not talking, Enos."

Enos evaded the professor's point. "The bishop has decided that we will all hear John Hershberger's confession."

"Yes, I know. Sunday at services."

"Humility is the . . ."

"Yes, I know—the strongest virtue."

"No Professor. The most *beautiful* virtue."

"Is humility the most beautiful virtue to Hershberger?"

"Confession is the beginning of humility, Professor. Confession is just the beginning, and that's where John Hershberger will start again."

＊　＊　＊

Across the road, Mike and Caroline found the Erbs' grocery store open late. Hannah Erb was behind the cash drawer, waiting for three customers to make their purchases. Two rang out quickly and left, but the third lingered in the aisle for dried fruits and roasted nuts.

The interior of the store was lighted by two round skylights and six white-glowing propane mantles hanging from brass fixtures in the ceiling. Hannah's counter was a simple three-by-five plywood bench with an old crank-handle adding machine. On shelves behind Hannah were hats and bonnets. Down the aisles stood three floor-to-ceiling shelves, double sided, holding a wide array of dried and canned goods.

The flours were put up in clear plastic bags closed with twist ties. Higher up, the cereals were in ziplock bags. Dried fruits sat in barrels, with paper bags at hand. There were canned goods of the commercial variety—beans, carrots, peas, soups, fruit, and syrups—and local goods put up in glass jars by neighbors—fruits, vegetables of every description, jams, jellies, and peanut butter. The Erbs also sold a few household goods—brooms, clothespins, coffee filters, and can openers. In one corner they even had a display of kitchen utensils.

After the last customer had left the store, Caroline stood near the door and let the professor walk around. He found a ladder on wheels, the top hooked to a metal track, like a library ladder. He pushed it to the end of the aisle and climbed up to reach a plastic sack of oatmeal. At the top, he was nearly six feet off the ground, and the ladder was unstable.

The professor paid for the oatmeal. As Hannah made change, Caroline moved over to the counter behind her husband, and the professor said, "Hannah, this is my wife Caroline."

Hannah nodded bashfully and said, "Pleased to meet you." She did not smile.

Caroline said, "I hope your Albert is going to be fine, Mrs. Erb."

Hannah wrung her hands in her apron without replying. Her eyes would not meet Caroline's.

Gently, Caroline said, "We have no children."

Hannah looked up puzzled. Childless couples were rare in her world. She appeared to be wondering if it were possible—a childless couple.

Caroline saw her considering this possibility and explained, "I had miscarriages, Mrs. Erb. The children died."

Branden watched his wife's face for the signs of sorrow and regret he usually saw when she spoke of children. He saw none of that now; she had set her own sorrows aside. Caroline was reaching out to the other woman for a common bond.

Hannah Erb said, "I am sorry to hear that, Mrs. Branden." Her tone was sincere. It was conciliatory. The professor took his package of oatmeal and eased through the door, leaving Hannah and Caroline alone in the store. Then he sat behind the steering wheel of the Miata and waited.

* * *

It was forty-five minutes before Caroline came out with Hannah. The two were talking about Albert, and as they passed the Miata in the parking lot, Caroline gave her husband a little "stay put" wave.

The women crossed the drive and took the sidewalk back beside the big house, going up the steps of the back porch and into the mudroom. The professor decided to stretch his legs.

* * *

Daniel Erb had been watching from the corner of the big house since the Brandens' Miata had driven up and parked in front of the family's store. He had seen the two Englishers go in and had taken the opportunity to move to the back corner of the store, where he could see the sports car better. And as the Brandens talked with *die Memme* inside the store, he studied the beautiful machine from his close perspective, his imagination roaming to the curvy, hilly stretches of blacktop, where he'd let that machine have all the speed it could handle. Where he'd go a hundred miles an hour and catch a glimpse of the world in a flash-by blur, taking corners like a wild man, daring fate on the crest of every hill.

That was his dream—to master the English gadgets one at a time. To take hold of the ultimate gadget, and make it roar. To tame a fine sports car and make it do his bidding.

The other gadgets were trifles by comparison, he thought. The library had computers, but he'd tired of those eventually. Cell phones had been fun, but only for a spell. Movies were just entertainment, no more exciting than the fantasies of his own mind. But the sports car! That was the ultimate challenge!

When Daniel saw the professor walk toward the barns at the back of the property, he slipped around the corner of the store, crept up to the blue machine, opened the driver's door, and sat behind the wheel.

He dare not let his feet touch the pedals. The knobs, dials, and panels were unfamiliar to him. But he understood the gear shifter and the steering wheel, and he caressed the wheel with his left hand and took hold of the shifter with his right. Then, making his best engine "grrr–ing" sound, he turned the wheel back and forth on the curves in his mind, and shifted so expertly that the roadster never lost speed.

* * *

When Caroline came out the front door, the professor was seated on a porch swing. Behind Caroline came Hannah, carrying Albert. Where his shaved scalp had been white before, Albert now had a faint gray stubble, his black hair already starting to grow in. Hannah set Albert down on his feet. The four-year-old stepped around to stand behind her legs and clung to her long skirt.

Without allowing him to say a word, Caroline pulled Branden off the swing and down the porch steps.

* * *

"He hasn't spoken," Caroline said, "and he closes his eyes when men are around." They were in the Miata, top down, heading home on Route 241 to Millersburg.

"But he opens his eyes to Hannah," she said. "He responds to her, Michael. I think he laughed inside, when she made a face for him. I could see that in his eyes. But his face shows no other emotions. His face is as blank as a wall. I don't think he'll ever be a little boy again."

Turning the corner at Mt. Hope, Branden pulled into the lot at Mrs. Yoder's Kitchen and parked near the door. The engine of a tour bus was growling down by the fence. Inside the restaurant, a crowd of tourists in the front hallway waited for tables. Branden caught the eye of the cashier, and she showed them to a small table in the corner nearest the kitchen. Coffee was delivered automatically.

"I'm not all that hungry," the professor said to the waitress. "Just the salad bar."

Caroline said, "Salad bar, too, please," and the little Amish waitress wrote out a slip and went to get water glasses.

As they ate, Caroline described what had happened inside the Erb house.

"First of all," she said, "all the men are gone. The whole district is over at Bishop Miller's house on Harrison Road."

Branden said, "I'd like to see that—there'll be twenty-five buggies parked on his front lawn."

"Albert was seated by himself at the big kitchen table. The other kids all had their chores, and they all stayed busy. Hannah sat me next to Albert, and he watched me like I was Russian—a Martian—somebody exotic. You'd have thought he had never seen an English woman. But I saw a little curiosity in his eyes. I saw him wondering about me."

"He didn't talk?" the professor asked.

"No, Michael. He uses his eyes. He let me see his eyes. Through his eyes, he let me see something that wasn't dead inside."

27

Monday, May 14
9:45 P.M.

THE HEADLIGHTS of the Miata brushed across the front of the Brandens' house and caught movement on the porch. The garage door was on its way up, but the professor canceled the remote and sent it back down. He immediately backed out into the cul-de-sac and trained the headlights on the front door.

Laura Pope, the college's chief registrar, turned from the doorbell and shielded her eyes from the headlights with a volume bound in senior thesis colors—brick red. She waved her free hand and called out, "Mike, I need to see you."

Caroline got out, and the professor pulled the Miata into the garage. Entering the house through the laundry room, he heard Pope saying to Caroline, "No, I can't stay."

Branden joined them in the vestibule. "What have you got there, Laura?"

She held out the thesis, saying, "This one needs a second look, Mike. I don't think it's worthy of a Millersburg College degree."

She handed the brick red volume to him, and he read the front cover. It was the thesis of Edwin Hunt-Myers III.

Branden again felt that weird, nervous compression in his spine. "What do you think is wrong with it?" he asked.

"I don't want to say," Pope answered, reaching back for the doorknob. "But would you read it, Mike? Give me your opinion?"

"Sure, but . . ."

Pope interrupted as she pulled the door open, "Please. Just read it. I trust you, Mike. If you say it's legitimate, I'll forget all about it. Frankly, I could stand to let it go. Then I might get some sleep."

*   *   *

"I've never seen Laura so rattled," the professor said to Caroline. They were in bed with the house locked up tight, security alarms activated. The house was peaceful, a haven from threat or danger. Eddie's thesis rested on the nightstand.

"Are you going to read it?" Caroline asked.

"She wants me to," Branden said.

"Why would she ask you to read a psych thesis?"

"I have no idea. Aidan Newhouse is Eddie's adviser, and Nina Lobrelli was the second reader. She thought Eddie's thesis was so good she nominated it for an award."

"What's Laura think you'll find?" Caroline asked.

"I don't know," the professor said, "but Laura Pope wouldn't come out to the house at this hour of the night unless she thought there was a real problem."

Tuesday, May 15
EARLY MORNING TO LATE AFTERNOON

EDDIE'S THESIS broke into the professor's dreams at four o'-clock the next morning. Still in his pajamas, he punched in numbers on the wall panel to turn off motion detectors on the first floor and took the thesis down to the kitchen to make coffee. While it brewed, he read the title:

Antisocial Behavior Disorder
in Christian Cults:
The Split of an Amish Church

At the kitchen table, the professor read Eddie's introduction, a review critical of authority abuse and cult submission inside the Branch Davidians at Waco, Texas, the Jim Jones People's Temple cult in Guyana, and The Family of Charles Manson. Eddie next presented the traits of classic personality and behavior disorders and moved straight from there to an assertion that the Amish constituted a Christian cult in Holmes County. He noted especially the singular authority of Amish bishops and the "blind, childlike submission of the congregants." He wrote about conformity among the Amish to arbitrary rules about dress, about the illogical spurning of modern devices, and about the backward and tragic reliance on folk medicine for diseases that were treatable with modern medicines. Eddie especially emphasized the "cruel practice of shunning" and commented that it seemed to him to be the least Christian of

140

all their practices, though in a *caveat* he wrote that he neither knew nor practiced Christianity himself. Finally, he argued that the Amish were a cult suitable for study and that his research would be designed to help a "modern and sophisticated public understand the nearly irresistible impulses at work among the subservient personalities in a patriarchal society."

Caroline called from the top of the steps. "Michael, what are you doing?"

He closed the thesis and went to the bottom of the steps. "I'm reading."

"Eddie's thesis?"

A sleepy nod.

"Come back to bed."

"In a minute."

* * *

At 6:45 A.M., Caroline came down to the kitchen and found her husband at the kitchen table, reading the last pages of Eddie's thesis. She checked the coffee and found it burned and stale, so she dumped it out and put up another pot. Then she sat across from her husband and waited.

When Branden had finished the thesis, she got up, poured two cups, and joined the professor, who had wandered out onto the back porch. He was slumped into a wicker chair, legs out straight and crossed at the ankles, and he had his arms folded over his chest. His eyes were closed in thought. When she placed a cup on the glass table next to his elbow, he mumbled, "I know why he did it," and went upstairs to get dressed.

* * *

"You know better, Aidan," Branden said. "You're not teaching them proper research methods. You taint their research with your own prejudices. It's not objective research."

"That's not fair, Mike!"

"You send them out after Koresh and Jim Jones, and then you aim them at the Amish. It casts bias into their work. Really Aidan, it's unprofessional."

"Look, Mike, I just ask them to think about the Amish from a new perspective. We're groundbreakers, Mike. It's new work. Original. Of course the Amish are a religious cult—they intermarry!"

"Cut the crap, Aidan. I've read the introduction of every senior thesis your students have written in the last ten years."

In fact, the professor had done just that. After a quick shower and breakfast, Branden had called the registrar and asked her to have Newhouse's students' thesis introductions and titles copied to a zip file and e-mailed to him at home. When he had the files, he extracted the documents and quickly scanned the titles. Then he read the introduction to each thesis. When he was sure of what he was seeing, he walked to campus and climbed to the second floor of the science building. There, he found Newhouse in his office and confronted him.

Newhouse argued, "Amish are a cult, Mike. Everybody gives them a pass because they're 'Christian.' Well, they're not *Christians*. Not proper ones, anyway. They're judgmental. They're homophobes and sexists. My God, the plight of the women alone ought to be enough to convince anyone."

"You're wrong, Aidan. And you're slipping. What's going on?"

Newhouse flushed crimson. He stared at Branden over his desk. His mind raced as he tried to gauge the level of his exposure. Of course one never read the entire thesis of every student. Not the better ones, anyway. It just took too much time. A thesis like Eddie Hunt-Myers's was a gift on a silver platter. He'd been one of the best. Sound research, well documented. Good writing, unusually expressive. Thorough treatment, referenced throughout. It had been nominated for the Walton Prize. Wait, stop, he thought. Perhaps that was a bit more exposure than was convenient. Thinking of other seniors who'd gotten an easy pass from him, Newhouse said,

"Mike, you can't throw a flag on a thesis like Eddie's. Of course I've read it. It's been nominated for the Walton."

"I know, Aidan," Branden said wearily. "I think that's gonna be a problem for us."

"Why?" Newhouse demanded.

"Again, Aidan, I think Eddie made it up."

"Made up what, precisely? What part?"

"The interviews he conducted with the Amish people, Aidan. I think his research is all a fabrication."

Newhouse groaned. "I've got all his recordings, Mike. They're on DVDs. I can't be expected to listen to all of them. You have any idea how many hours of conversation it takes to get usable research?"

Branden asked, "Did you really listen to any of them, Aidan?"

"A few. At first."

Branden waited.

Newhouse got to his feet and said, "I can't do this again, Mike. You understand? I went through this with my son."

"I know, Aidan," Branden said. "Maybe you'd better start checking those disks."

Newhouse's expression grew vacant, and Branden said, "Aidan, please check the research. I think Eddie made it all up."

Slowly, Professor Newhouse brought his gaze back into focus. He looked at Branden and said, "I can't do this again."

*   *   *

Branden made it to the registrar's office just as it was closing. The secretary showed him back to Laura Pope, and Branden found her standing at a west-facing window. He said, "Hi, Laura," as he entered, and she turned to him and said, "This is our big breather, Mike. Two days after commencement, and then it all starts up again."

"No rest for the wicked," Branden said.

"None at all."

"Listen, Laura, I read Eddie's thesis. Could you pull his folder?"

"Don't have to," Pope said. "That one I know by heart."

"Why's that?"

"When he first got here, Arne Laughton told me he was special."

"Oh?"

"Mike, he has fifteen more transfer credits than the Statute of Instruction allows."

"You still cleared him for graduation?"

"I didn't. Arne did."

"OK, but why do you know his folder so well?"

"He's used every excuse, angle, and fudge factor there is. Got a D changed to a B⁻. Turned in tardy work to cover 'Incompletes.' Took medical withdrawals for any class he was failing, and brought us signed documentation for credit-bearing internships that I don't believe he actually finished. He's the biggest excuse maker I've ever known. He wants exceptions and special handling for everything. I've tried to pin him down a time or two, but it's like nailing Jell-O to the ceiling."

Branden stroked his beard and thought about Eddie's thesis. "He takes shortcuts a lot, Laura?"

"In the extreme, Mike."

"We accepted his thesis?"

"On Aidan Newhouse's word. Because Arne Laughton backed him up."

"And you don't like this kid."

"I don't like it, Mike, when people think they're so special that they don't have to follow the rules."

29

Tuesday, May 15
5:20 P.M.

BRANDEN FOUND Dr. Nina Lobrelli still in her tattered white
lab coat, standing beside her bookshelves, reading a biochemistry
monograph. He cleared his throat, and she looked up.

"Nina, I need to see your chart," Branden said without preamble.

Lobrelli asked, "Which one? Our isoxazolidine activators?"

"Not the science, Nina. The genealogy."

Lobrelli seemed disappointed not to be able to talk about her research. "It's in the teaching lab," she said and led him across the hall.

A wide sheet of professional poster paper, three feet by six feet,
had been taped to the brick wall and most of a chalkboard. It had
been printed on a large format printer, using several colors of ink,
and it showed the genealogy of at least six generations of Amish
families related to the Erbs. Mostly, there were Erbs, Weavers,
Klines, and Hershbergers. Clearly, in some cases, cousins had married each other, and these names were printed in green ink. Then,
among their descendants, any genetic disorder was noted paren-
thetically in red. Because of close-relative marriages, the clan was
afflicted by a marked predominance of a rare and aggressive form of
psoriasis. There also were more than the usual number of cases of
Parkinson's. And there were the dwarves Benny and Enos, plus one
of Enos's children, a dwarf boy of seventeen years, plus one dwarf
grandparent of Enos and two dwarves among distant relatives.

"When was this printed?" Branden asked.

Lobrelli checked a small number in the lower right corner. "May 11th. Friday."

"How often do you revise it?"

"The students do that. Every month or so, I guess. Whenever there's a birth."

"Do you think it's complete, Nina? Is this the whole clan?"

"It's all the people who trace back to Joshua and Annie Weaver."

"Does it show family members who've moved out of the county?"

"I think so. The students put this together using their interviews, so they got it all directly from the Amish people out there."

"And you got started with Benny? He was your first contact in this family?"

"Yes. Benny Erb. I met him in Aidan's office on the second floor. Maybe a year ago. Aidan suggested a genealogy chart might be interesting, and I put Cathy Billett on it."

"Do you have this on disk?" Branden asked, tapping the paper.

"I don't, but I'm sure one of the students does."

"Any of them staying here for the summer?"

"No, just my research students."

Branden fished out his phone and asked, "Can I take a picture of part of this?"

"Shoot the whole thing if you like, Mike."

The professor started taking pictures, saying, "I just need this corner."

*   *   *

Back home, Branden printed the photos he'd taken and taped the several pages together to make a layout on the kitchen table of one corner of Lobrelli's genealogy chart.

Caroline asked, "What's that?" and the professor explained, "It's part of a genealogy chart. I got it from Nina. Here's Benny and Enos Erb, the dwarf sons of Annie and Samuel Erb. Enos told me about some of this when he first came to see me. This is a chart of his whole family."

"Does he know Lobrelli has everything charted out like this?"

"Don't know."

"What's the connection?"

"Benny Erb is the connection. Benny the chatterbox."

* * *

That evening, the professor read Eddie's interview data out loud from Eddie's thesis, and Caroline circled each name on the genealogy chart that seemed to correspond with a description in the thesis. They were guessing at first about the names, but became more sure of their identifications with each instance of overlap. Eddie had been careful to state in his thesis that he had changed the names to protect the anonymity of the people he had interviewed. He insisted, though, that the people were real, and the Brandens found that there was a clear and direct correspondence between case subjects in Eddie's interviews and the descriptions or physical ailments of the real people on Lobrelli's genealogy chart. The dwarf brothers Enos and Benjamin were not named, but they were clearly suggested by Eddie's description of the families living across the road from one another. And in the results section of his thesis, Eddie had included transcriptions of the interviews he had recorded with each subject in the district, which he purported to be a word-for-word record of what was said to him about the pending split in the congregation.

Eddie claimed that the people at Calmoutier had described the alarming anger and discord that had bloomed in their congregation over the use of modern medicines. Eddie reported case after case of brothers who were no longer speaking, children who could no longer visit their parents, cousins who would not correspond with one another, businesses ruined because of a shunning, and discord over increasingly minor matters, until the congregation had split, half following the old bishop, an Anti, and the other half following a Modern. It was a persuasive collection of evidence, and Branden knew it was all a profane lie.

Nothing so severe as this had happened in Benny's church. Nothing of the kind ever would. The people were all very real, but not one of them could have talked with Eddie Hunt-Myers. Not one of them could have behaved in such an angry and bitter way. The stories of anger, bordering on rage and spitefulness, could not be true. The discord perhaps existed, but not the extreme level of hostility that Eddie described.

Caroline listened to the professor's explanation and said, "Get Cal to listen to this. Maybe you're wrong."

"I'm not wrong," Branden said.

"Talk to Cal, Michael. He knows that whole family."

"I'm right, Caroline. All the circles you put on that chart are a match to someone in Eddie's thesis. They all match."

"Then how did Eddie have this kind of personal detail about all of them? How'd he know so much?"

"My guess is he had a phone pal."

"Benny?"

"Benny Erb was a chatterbox, by everybody's description. He was a very sociable chatterbox, who gave Eddie Hunt-Myers a ready-made thesis, without any actual work."

"Then it's all made up, Michael."

"Right. Benny gave Eddie accurate descriptions of all the people, and then Eddie made up the interviews to suit his needs. To satisfy Aidan's biases and portray the Amish as haters."

"What are you going to do about it?"

"I'm gonna catch Eddie Hunt-Myers before he leaves town."

"What are you going to do about Newhouse?"

"That I haven't decided."

30

Tuesday, May 15
8:30 P.M.

THE PRESIDENT'S mansion was a sprawling brick structure with a dozen angled rooflines, an assortment of spires and crests, wrought-iron trellises, and two large chimneys at either end. It sat on elaborately landscaped grounds at the edge of the athletic fields, on the north side of campus. Flower gardens, brick walkways, flagstone patios, and large expanses of lawn surrounded the house. The oval driveway was lighted at night by powerful halogen bulbs on tall aluminum poles, and the front face of the house was washed with floodlights mounted on concrete pads on the ground.

When Branden rang the doorbell, lights were burning in nearly every window of the house, and cars were parked both in the semicircular drive and out at the curb. A pudgy gentleman in a tuxedo answered the door with a smile. He held the door open and said, "Come in, Professor," in an affected, supercilious tone.

Branden laughed. When the president entertained, the head of food services at the college always worked the door with an accent and an attitude so far removed from the real, down-home Bill Taylor that people who knew him just laughed.

Past a smile that was stretching his cheeks, Branden said, "Bill, I need to talk to Arne."

"He's in the study."

"Please ask him to come out, Bill. It's important."

With a conspirator's smile, Bill asked, "May I bring you a drink?"

"Just the president, please. Tell him it's about Eddie Hunt-Myers. I'll wait outside."

Bill gave a curt nod and a stage bow and disappeared into the house. When Arne Laughton came out, he was carrying two glasses of red wine. He handed one to Branden and complained, "I'm working on the endowment, Mike. Can't this wait?"

Branden took the stemmed glass, saying, "I'm afraid it can't, Arne. Time is critical." Laughton grumbled but allowed Branden to lead him down the lighted drive and into a small rose garden in front of the house, where the lights of the driveway did not shine.

"Arne, I need you to keep the Hunt-Myers family in town for another day."

Laughton sipped some wine and said, "Too late, Mike. They all left after dinner."

Branden pulled the president farther into the rose garden. "Arne, Eddie Hunt-Myers didn't do his own research. He made up most of it. Maybe all of it."

Skeptical, Laughton asked, "What are you talking about?"

"Eddie's thesis is about the split in the Amish community out at Calmoutier. I think he used an Amish fellow to get the details for all the people he described in his thesis. And for all the genealogical background on the families, where he says he conducted deep interviews."

"I saw that thesis, Mike. It's two hundred pages long."

"And one hundred and seventy-five pages of it are clever fabrications, Arne."

"Why would he do that?"

"Doesn't matter, Arne. Maybe he's lazy. Maybe he likes the thrill. But the thesis is a fabrication. The interviews are fake. I think I can prove it."

"These are big donors, Mike—the Hunt-Myerses. You can't accuse their son of something like this. We just handed him a diploma, for heaven's sake."

"Are the Billetts still in town, Arne?"

"I don't know."

"Are they big donors, too, Arne?"

"Not really. They're threatening to sue us."

"Because the tower wasn't locked?"

"It was locked, Mike."

"They're going to argue it wasn't, Arne, you've got to be able to see that. How do you think Eddie and Cathy got up there?"

"Did you talk to the Billetts, Mike? Did the Billetts tell you they were going to sue us?"

"No."

"No, what?"

"Neither. Look, Arne, I think Eddie's responsible for Cathy's death."

"Mike! You've got to stop this!"

"Do you know about the two little Amish kids who were kidnapped Saturday?"

"A little. I've been busy. You know how commencement weekend is. It's the last chance I'll have to get a donation from some of those families."

"I think the Amish are the key to Cathy's murder, Arne."

"Stop! Just stop, Mike. You can't be serious."

"Eddie's thesis is a fraud, Arne. That's the linchpin."

"Wait just a minute. I took the Billetts down to see Missy, myself. I was there."

A guest at the party stepped out onto the driveway and lit a cigarette. Laughton drew Branden around the corner of the mansion and finished in a whisper. "Missy says there's no way to prove Cathy Billett's death wasn't a suicide."

"I know some of the people who were supposedly interviewed for Eddie's thesis, Arne. They're real people, but there's no way they can have said those things. Eddie made up something that'd satisfy Aidan Newhouse, and he turned it in for his thesis. But he never conducted a single interview."

Laughton stared hard in the dark at Branden, shook his head, and said, "You can't be serious. What proof do you have?"

"I don't really have any, Arne. But the two children who were kidnapped can't speak yet, and their uncle Benny conveniently fell off a ladder three weeks ago."

"Who?"

"Benny Erb, Arne. He's dead, too."

"Really, Mike. You need to take a couple of months to relax and settle your nerves. This is preposterous. You're just plain nuts if you think I'm going to confront the Hunt-Myerses over something like this. For crying out loud, Mike, we just graduated their kid!"

*   *   *

While walking home in the dark, the professor called Missy Taggert's number and said, "Sorry about the late call."

Missy called over her shoulder, "Bruce, it's Mike. I'll be outside." Then she said, "It's fine, Mike. We were just reading."

"Missy, I need to know if there's any way Benny Erb and Cathy Billett can have been murdered."

"You think they were?" Missy asked.

"Maybe. Can we tell for sure, one way or the other?"

"There's no way to know, Mike. I told you that. They both looked like falls. But are you thinking they were pushed? Why, exactly?"

"I don't know. Did you find anything on the clothes from Albert Erb? Any evidence of the kidnapper?"

"No. Is Albert OK?"

"Not really. Maybe, I'm not sure. Caroline spoke to him. She thinks he's got a chance."

"The clothes gave us nothing, Mike. And I tried everything I could think of."

"No hair? Oils? Nothing like that?"

"It doesn't work like TV, Mike. How about little Mattie?"

"No change, Missy. Look, what if we went back out to the woods? What if we missed something there?"

"We could try."

"Would you?"

"I'll go back tomorrow."

"Ask Bruce to give you some help."

"Won't be a problem, Mike. But what are you thinking here? This looks like three separate things to me. It looks like an accidental death, a suicide, plus the kidnappings."

"I think it's all related, Missy. I think a fraudulent student thesis is the link to everything."

"You going to be able to prove any of that?"

"Not at this rate," Branden said. "Probably not in this life."

* * *

At home, the professor found Caroline preparing for bed. He propped up several pillows and stretched his legs out on the bed, but couldn't find comfort. Abandoning the bedroom, he went into his study, but there he was still restless. He tried the soft chair. He tried the desk chair. He couldn't relax.

Caroline followed, tying her blue terrycloth bathrobe around her waist. "Did you find Eddie?"

"He left for Florida with his family," the professor said. He stood in front of the window to stare out at the streetlights. "I need to take a photograph of Eddie out to the Erbs. See if Albert or Mattie can recognize him."

Caroline said, "The only thing you've really got, Michael, are suspicions about his thesis."

"They might recognize him," Branden said, falling behind Caroline's remark.

"You'll harm them if you do that," she said emphatically.

"Then you're right," the professor said. "I've got nothing but suspicions."

"I still think you should call Cal about this, Michael."

The professor considered that suggestion while he mulled over the evidence. In the end, he admitted that he really didn't have any evidence. Suspicions, yes. But not evidence.

There was the thesis—a fabrication? Probably. There were also the two deaths—murders? Probably not. He saw Mattie in the woods, struggling against her bindings, and Albert in his father's arms, squeezing his eyes shut as tightly as he could manage. OK, Professor, he thought. Toss out Cathy Billett. Maybe she jumped, like Eddie said. Maybe Eddie had been cruel to her, so she jumped. But if Eddie had actually killed Benny Erb, he would have done everything he could to have stopped her. He would have talked her back from the edge, because a second suspicious death was not what Eddie would have needed right then. It was the last thing he would have wanted.

But the kidnappings, Branden thought, were still a problem. Did Eddie do that? Why would he need to? What would he gain?

In his memory, he saw Enos standing on the front steps of his house. "Confession is the start of humility," he had said. John Hershberger's confession. For what? What had Hershberger done?

A new thought occurred to him. Maybe that was it. Did it make any sense at all? Hershberger was set to be bishop in a new district. He was prepared to take all of the Moderns out of Andy Miller's church and start a new congregation. But not now. Something had changed that. Confession. Why the need?

And the children had been released by their abductor. Why? What did the Amish have that the kidnapper—Eddie Hunt-Myers —would want?

Branden pulled his cell phone out, punched in Cal Troyer's number, and asked, "You asleep, Cal?"

Troyer laughed. "No, I've been out at Calmoutier most of the day. Came home and couldn't sleep. So I'm up trying to write a letter."

"Cal, I talked to Enos Erb yesterday. He told me John Hershberger is not going to split that congregation after all. Is that right?"

"Right, he's not," Cal said. "Andy Miller is letting him stay if he confesses and repents."

"This Sunday?" Branden asked.

"It's all set up. Everybody knows about it."

"Cal, I want you to take me to visit Bishop Andy Miller."

"When, Sunday?"

"No. Tomorrow, Cal."

"OK, that shouldn't be a problem."

"It might be, once I talk with him."

Cal asked, "Why? What's going on?"

"Bishop Miller, Cal. I want him to put a stop to the whole thing."

31

Wednesday, May 16
9:30 A.M.

BISHOP ANDY MILLER lived on Harrison Road, just over the
Wayne County border, about a mile east of the Schlabaughs' fur-
niture store. His house was a new, simple wood-frame box of two
stories, with steep rooflines and green shingles. There was a sitting
porch off the second-floor bedrooms and a clothesline strung
under the porch, at ground level. All the usual absences of an Amish
home were in evidence—no electric or cable service, no phone lines,
no fancy garage, and no cars. In the front yard, Miller had five purple martin houses perched atop tall wooden poles, and on the hill
behind a red bank barn stood a new aluminum windmill, silver
blades turning slowly against a blue morning sky.

Cal pulled his gray truck up to the side of the house, shut off his
engine, and waited in polite Amish fashion for Miller to come out.
Professor Branden sat restlessly in the passenger's seat, wanting to
walk up to the house and knock on the door. He had his hand on
his door handle when Miller appeared around the back corner of
the house.

The bishop was a short, balding man. His chin whiskers were
gray and bushy, and he wore wire spectacles. His denim clothes were
old and worn, and his black vest was undone in front. The sleeves
of his blue shirt were rolled to precisely the approved location on
his arm, just a little below his elbows. When Branden pulled him-

self out of Cal's truck, Miller offered his hand, pumped the shake once with firmness, and led the men to the back.

Miller's wife served coffee to the men on a back patio with a picnic table. Cal listened while the professor sat across from the bishop and asked polite questions about Albert and Mattie. Polite questions about Enos and Israel. About Hershberger's rebellion and subsequent capitulation.

Miller answered all of the professor's questions calmly and carefully. When Branden asked him to postpone the Sunday confession of John Hershberger, Miller's gaze turned sadly inward. He smiled like a reluctant sage and studied the redwood boards of the picnic table. When he turned his eyes up to Branden's, he spoke slowly, deliberately, as if the sanctity of the whole congregation rested on how he answered this particular question.

"If we don't do it, Professor," Miller asked, "who will keep the old ways? If we Amish don't keep the old ways, who will? And what is the new? Should a bishop tolerate any new doctrine? Should I allow the people to go out into any part of the English world they choose? Any part at all, Professor? Shall I tell a mother and a wife that it is acceptable to spend two hours a day at an exercise spa to lose weight, when her family waits at home? What shall guide my decisions?"

Branden tipped his head to acknowledge the questions without answering.

"The people need authority, Professor. How else are they to understand the difficulties of the *Bauern,* the peasants? And does God ask of us more than a life of simple peasant farming?

"But a man will think he knows better than a bishop. He rehearses his reasons and thinks himself better. To do so is prideful, Professor. It is the start of a great fall.

"Others lose strength when this happens. Their sufferings, then, do not make them godly. They only make them miserable. Here is where Grace is most diminished, because we all must suffer. God promises that we will suffer for a reason—to make us whole. If we try to fix everything to lessen our sufferings, we deny our relationship with God. We deny our dependence.

"So, we Amish accept our disabilities. To do otherwise is to rebel against God's authority. Our lives are supposed to be hard. We do not flee this truth. We trust that nothing can harm us that God has not allowed. Should a short man blame God? Should sorrow diminish our faith?

"John Hershberger knows these things. He was raised to honor them. He will repent at Sunday services because he accepts the authority God has instituted among us. I cannot postpone his repentance. I too must submit to God.

"Do you understand, Professor? This binds us to one another. This is what makes us whole. Nowhere else is faith more strong than in submission."

Branden did not interrupt. He knew he had his answer. He had thought a postponement would help give him time. Time to work on the one thing that would best give Albert and Mattie a chance to heal. But Hershberger himself had set the clock on this, and the clock was running. By this time Sunday morning, Hershberger's secret would be spoken aloud. And if Eddie Hunt-Myers had done this to Albert and Mattie, then confession was the one thing Eddie couldn't allow.

Branden struggled for a way to explain this to Miller. He struggled to match English justice with Amish fatalism, and he felt certain he would fail. Still, he wanted to ask the question that most troubled him about Amish pacifism. "What then, Bishop Miller, of people like Mattie and Albert, who are victims of evil men? Where is the protection for the children? How does your leadership give them safety? Or give them peace? And what do you say of the kidnapper who took the children?"

Miller smiled as if he appreciated the irony of the question. He smiled as if he had answered these questions for himself on a daily basis for as long as he had lived. "You are troubled for the children?" he said. "I understand. But, we are nonresisters, Professor Branden. We take pacifism to the next level and will not resist verbal or physical attacks of any kind. As for safety, only God can provide for us."

Miller held off Branden's response with a raised hand. "We know from the long persecutions our ancestors endured in Europe that we are powerless to stand against evil. We do not resist. To do so would add violence to violence, and the sin of this would then be ours. Answer this question for me, Professor. We do not understand. How can English be opposed to abortion but in favor of war? Or how can English be opposed to war but in favor of abortion? Are these not both killing?"

Branden nodded to say he acknowledged the point. He asked, "Then, Bishop Miller, what of the people who do evil against you? Is there no justice as far as you're concerned?"

Miller stroked his beard. He spoke with the voice of deep conviction. "What is justice?" he asked. "It is nothing in this world. No, it is testimony alone that matters, Professor. An evil person has testified about himself, because every act of life is testimony. We all testify with our lives. That testimony is laid down as an historical record in the linear realm of time, but our testimony is lodged also in the infinite realm of eternity, where it stands as a witness of what we thought, said, and did. From the viewpoint of eternity, the condition of our hearts is assessed by God, as we testify about ourselves. As our lives are written in the record of eternity. Based on this assessment, our lives are judged by God, who is solely capable of doing this. There is, therefore, no escaping who we are and what we have done. Our lives follow us into eternity. We let God judge us all. We are content to accept His judgment. We let God judge the hearts of evil men, because He alone is qualified to do it."

Branden considered what the bishop had said, taking his time to understand it. Giving it the appreciation it deserved. In the end, he could ask only one thing of the man. "May I attend Sunday services?"

The bishop smiled and said, "Yes, Professor. Have Pastor Troyer bring you out."

Cal asked, "Which farm, Andy?"

"John Hershberger's, Cal. We'll be at John Hershberger's barn, on Nisley Road."

32

Wednesday, May 16
11:25 A.M.

PROFESSOR NATHAN WELLS had kept the same ritual for thirty-five years. On the days after commencement, he sat on a bench in the oak grove each morning at 11:00 and read the senior thesis of each of his students who had died. He spent an hour at it each day and continued until he was done. Only foul weather kept him home. This year, he had five to read, plus an essay Cathy Billett had written for him as a sophomore. It wasn't a thesis, but it was all he had of hers.

It was his habit to go through the students in order, starting with Able Sayers, who had committed suicide the day before commencement, at the end of Professor Wells's first year of teaching. The count had held at five for the last twelve years. Besides Able Sayers, there had been two deaths from cancer, one in the first Iraq war, and one in a car crash in Boston. To have added Cathy Billett's memory to his devotions had been nearly the limit of what Nathan Wells could bear.

Branden found him on his bench with his eyes closed, Cathy Billett's essay lying open in his lap. When Branden sat down, Wells gently folded the pages and said, "It's too hard, Mike. I can't read them anymore."

Branden said, "I didn't know Cathy had written for you, Nate."

Wells took a long look at Billett's paper and handed it to Branden, saying, "It's her final essay from my class on lesser-known

American cultures. I told Arne Laughton this morning that I've retired, Mike. Gave him my letter."

Branden nodded and smoothed his palm over the front of Billett's essay, saying, "I'll read them all for you, Nate, in your place. As long as I'm still here."

Wells took a calming breath but said only, "OK, Mike. I can't do it anymore."

Branden held his peace, letting the oak grove serve as witness to their covenant. After a few moments, he broke the silence. "Hope Elliot wrote her senior thesis for you this year."

Wells, staring inward at his own thoughts, seemed not to have heard.

"What can you tell me about her, Nate? About Hope Elliot."

Wells pulled himself back to the present. "Hope Elliot? Solid student. Bs for the most part. She had a rough patch early last semester, but she got over it. Then, Cathy Billett."

"They were friends?"

"Since Cathy's first year. Except this last semester, of course. They were roommates last year."

"Is Hope reliable, Nate?"

"On what topic?"

"Eddie Hunt-Myers."

"You're kidding."

"No. She told me something about Eddie. I need to know if she is reliable."

"She knows a lot about him, if that's what you're asking."

"I am."

"They were an item, those two—up until last semester. But Eddie had a lot of girlfriends. He traded them in like used cars."

"And how about Cathy Billett? What was her relationship to them?"

"She broke them up, Mike. Otherwise that would have been Hope up on the bell tower."

"He drove a wedge between Hope and Cathy?"

"Very much so. I told her 'good riddance.'"

"Hope?"

"Yes. I told her she was better off without him."

"So you know Eddie, too," Branden said, hoping to draw Professor Wells toward a comment about Eddie.

"Only had him for one class."

"I think Eddie is pretty smart, Nate."

"Too smart by half, Mike."

Branden waited for the explanation.

"Eddie got everything the first time. If he heard it or read it, he had it down pat. Never really had to study. Trouble is, nothing ever held his interest long enough for him to master it."

"Knew a little about everything, Nate?"

Wells nodded, "But not very much about anything."

"He did finish a thesis for Aidan Newhouse, Nate."

"Then that's the first thing he ever finished in his life."

33

Wednesday, May 16
1:30 P.M.

THE REGISTRAR had Hope Elliot's cell phone number, and when Branden rang it, she answered with a cautious, "Yes?"

"Hope Elliot?" Branden asked.

"Who's calling?"

"Professor Michael Branden."

Hope did not respond.

"Hope," Branden said, "I'm listening, now." He'd thought this through. It was the best thing he could say to gain her trust. "I want to hear about Eddie."

"It doesn't matter, Professor."

"Hope, it does. It matters a lot."

"Why?"

"I think his thesis is a fraud."

"I could have told you that."

"I also think he kidnapped two little Amish children. Last Saturday, Hope."

"They all right?"

"They're home, Hope, but they are not all right."

"He's got a stone for a heart, Professor. He doesn't care about anyone but himself. He hasn't got a single male friend in the whole world. And he hates his parents."

"Can you help me understand that, Hope?"

"I'll tell you several things about Eddie. He's rich. He'll never want for anything. But he takes what he wants, and he discards what he's tired of. He threw me over for Cathy Billett without so much as a word to me. But before that, one night last October, he told me what he wanted out of life. I don't know why he did, because Eddie hides his real nature most of the time. But he told me that night what he dreamed of most. I think he wanted to see shock in me. To see shock in my eyes, because that's what he did when he told me—he looked so deep into my eyes that it felt like rape. He said his biggest dream in life was that his parents would be killed in a plane crash, and he'd inherit everything they have. How's that for cold ambition, Professor? He would trade his family for a boatyard."

Branden was stunned. It took him several long seconds to speak, then he said, "Hope, I want you to tell me again why you think he killed Cathy Billett."

Silence from Hope Elliot.

"Hope? Are you still there?"

"Yes."

Branden waited. He let time fill the connection.

Eventually, Hope said, "He called me yesterday, Dr. Branden."

"Eddie?"

"He said he wants us to hook up again."

"I hope you're not considering that."

"No, Professor. But that's not what he meant."

"Did he threaten you, Hope?"

"It was a threat just to hear his voice. He wanted me to know he can find me. I think he was laughing to himself when he spoke. You know—laughing that he's so clever."

"What did you tell him?"

"I told him he could take a long jump off a short pier, for all I cared."

Branden chuckled and didn't try to hide it. "I think you're safe, Hope. He's gone back to Florida."

This time it was Hope Elliot who let a silent pause fill the connection.

"Hope?" Branden asked.

"Professor Branden, the number he called from had a 330 area code."

"He didn't use his cell phone?"

"I'd never have taken his call if I'd recognized his number. No, I think he called from a land line. But it was area code 330. The rest I don't remember."

"Check your phone records for incoming calls, Hope. That number will be there."

"I deleted it, Professor. Didn't want the call on my phone. Don't want the creep in my head."

"You going to be OK, Hope? Safe? At least until I can sort this out?"

"I'm in Montana. Flew out here with Cathy's parents yesterday."

"Does Eddie know where that is? The Billett ranch?"

"I think so."

"Then be careful."

"Don't worry, Professor. The ranch hands out here all carry guns."

34

Wednesday, May 16
5:45 P.M.

WHEN MISSY TAGGERT showed up at the Brandens' front door, Bruce Robertson was with her, and he was carrying two large pizzas. Caroline had started on a dinner salad, so she served that on the back porch, with the pizza. The four talked while they ate.

Missy said, "We went back out to the woods at Calmoutier, Mike. Didn't find a thing."

Branden shook his head. "I need something to link Eddie Hunt-Myers to this. I need something more than suspicions."

Robertson said, "There, we may be able to help you," and took a second slice. "I attended a seminar at Quantico—the FBI—last fall. It was about profiling criminal personalities. Developing an understanding of the types of personalities who commit these crimes, like kidnappings, torture, and murder. So, Missy and I were wondering, what kind of person could kidnap two little Amish kids like that, and use a butchered puppy to paralyze them with fear?"

Missy asked, "Mike, this Eddie. Is he a loner, or a joiner?"

Branden said, "One of his former girlfriends told me he's definitely a loner."

Missy took another slice and asked, "He a finisher or a quitter?"

"Nate Wells says he never really finished anything. Lost interest too fast."

"Confident and forward, or hesitating and retiring?"

Caroline answered, "I think he's overly confident."

Missy asked, "Why?"

"He gave Michael a copy of his letter of apology to the Billetts. Asked him to read it and to help improve it. But I think he was playing us for fools."

"That's what's so baffling," the professor said. "There's no reason for him to have done that."

"He wanted you to think he's a dunce," Missy said.

"I suppose so," Branden said.

"Was his mother at commencement, Mike?"

"Yes."

"Notice anything between them?"

"Like what?"

"A special glance? Maybe a weird familiarity. Something between them that shouldn't be there."

"His smile, when he hugged her," Branden said.

"What about it?"

"Didn't seem right, somehow."

Missy nodded thoughtfully and asked, "Does he switch from girl to girl a lot, or has he kept a long-standing relationship with anyone?"

The professor said, "He's had too many girlfriends. He dumps one and moves to another. Doesn't seem to faze him."

"It fits, Missy," the sheriff said.

Caroline said, "What? What fits?"

Missy laid her slice of pizza back in the box and said, "It's a certain personality type. I think Eddie could have done this—kidnapped the children. I think he's the type."

"What?" Branden asked, eyebrows raised.

Bruce said, "He's got no follow-through, Mike. A short attention span. He's cruel to people who love him, like Cathy Billett. He likes his thrills—writing an apology to the Billetts and then asking you to read it. He's got an outgoing personality, but no real friendships. He has trouble with long-term relationships. He's a loner, really. And if Missy's right about those kidnappings, then he's got no soul. No sense of remorse. He could have done that and never felt a thing. And I'd bet there's something going on with his mother. That's the profile of an intelligent sociopath."

"I don't like who you're describing," Caroline said. "It's creepy."

"What exactly are you two saying?" Branden asked.

Missy said, "It's possible he's just antisocial at a criminal level, but he may also be borderline psychopathic."

"He's insane?" Caroline asked.

"Insane is probably not the right word," Missy said. "For one thing, he's not out of control. He probably understands himself quite well, although he may be somewhat delusional about his motives. He may not be able to appreciate the consequences of all of his actions, and he may not be much of a forward thinker. He probably has a poor understanding of 'the future.' But he knows what he wants, and he always knows what he is doing. So, he's not 'insane.' But that's what makes him so dangerous."

Caroline said, "At least he's back in Florida now."

Cautiously, Branden said, "I'm not so sure about that anymore."

"Do you know where he is?" the sheriff asked.

Branden reluctantly shook his head. "Somewhere in Holmes County, Bruce. He made a phone call from right here in Holmes County."

35

Wednesday, May 16
6:30 P.M.

ROBERTSON TOOK his phone out, called Ed Hollings, the night dispatcher down at the jail, and spoke with urgency. "Ed, I want you to put it out to everyone, and I mean right now, that we're looking for Mr. Eddie Hunt-Myers, who just graduated from Millersburg. Right, wait. Mike, we need your best description."

"Six feet, maybe six-one. Two hundred pounds, give or take, blond hair, blue eyes, southern accent. He's strong—built solid."

"Did you get that, Ed? OK, now this kid is wanted for questioning in the two Amish kidnappings. He's to be considered dangerous, and he may be armed. A knife that I know of. Don't know about guns. Right, Ed. Right now—to everyone. Coordinate this with Wayne County, too."

Branden said, "The Erbs, Bruce. Protect the Erbs."

"Ed, send two units out to the two Erb farms on Nisley Road. Ricky Niell knows the addresses. OK, so call in the day shifts. No, both of them. I want this guy found." He switched off.

Branden said, "You've pegged this a little higher than I had it."

Robertson shook his head. "If he's sociopathic, maybe even just antisocial, then he's the type of person who would have kidnapped those two kids. That's what got us started on this—asking what kind of person could do that."

Branden argued, "But, *why* would he do that? I still can't figure out the reason."

"It's so simple," Caroline said softly. She set her salad bowl down and seemed miserable to be thinking such troubling thoughts. "It's the phone."

"What?" Branden asked.

"This only makes sense," Caroline said, "if Eddie did it all. If that's true, then he killed Benny Erb, expecting to recover the cell phone he had given to him. Well, he didn't get if back by killing Benny, so he kidnapped the children, and John Hershberger took Eddie's call on Benny's phone. Israel Erb had given it to Hershberger after he took it from his daughter. Eddie would have called again and told Hershberger that he'd trade Albert for the phone, and Hershberger must have agreed. That's why Eddie released Albert. He got what he wanted. Hershberger gave him Benny's phone. That's the phone Eddie originally gave to Benny, so he could ask Benny about the families out at Calmoutier. Eddie wanted the phone back, Michael. That's what makes it all fit."

The professor was stunned into silence. Robertson opened his phone and called Ed Hollings again. "Ed, Bruce. We also want to question a John Hershberger."

Branden interrupted, "He's got a farm on Nisley Road, too."

"Nisley Road, Ed. Put Armbruster on this. I want Hershberger in my office by morning."

Branden said, "I believed Hershberger when he said he had burned the phone. I believed him! But he lied to me. He lied to everyone about that, and that's what his confession will be on Sunday. That's why he's been called to repent—he lied about burning that phone."

* * *

They were working on a list of first-search locations in Holmes County, places to start the hunt for Eddie, when the doorbell rang. Caroline went to answer it, while Branden, Robertson, and Taggert finished the list.

Caroline brought Nina Lobrelli to the back porch, saying, "Mike, you're going to want to hear this."

Lobrelli took off a light jacket, threw it over a chair, and sat down heavily. "I just came from Aidan Newhouse's office," she said, starting to shake. "Ben Capper is with him. He's hung himself."

Branden and Robertson stood up together, and Branden asked, "When, Nina? Just now?"

Professor Lobrelli nodded and sank further into the chair.

From somewhere near the center of town came the siren of a sheriff's cruiser. At nearly the same time, Robertson's phone squawked, and he took the call, listened, and said, "Yeah, Ed. We just got that."

Branden said, "What?"

Robertson switched off, took a long look at Professor Lobrelli, and said, "Your Ben Capper just called it in. Professor Newhouse is hanging from a light fixture in his office."

36

Wednesday, May 16
9:10 P.M.

WITHIN THE HOUR, the sheriff had his whole investigative team in the office of Professor Aidan Newhouse. Newhouse was cut down, still wearing Ben Capper's cuffs on one wrist. Deputy Pat Lance was dusting the office for prints, and Dan Wilsher had Lobrelli out in the hall, going over her account of finding Newhouse. Ben Capper stood down the hall, arms folded somberly over his chest.

Missy stood up beside the body and pulled off her blue nitrile gloves. "If this was suicide," she said, "he changed his mind. He's got deep gouges at his neck, where he tried to pull the noose off, and he's got fingernails broken off in the rope."

Robertson asked, "Can it also have been murder, Missy?"

"Yes. Either he kicked that chair over there and did it himself, or someone clever laid this scene out to look like that's what he did."

Robertson stepped out into the hall, made a call, and spoke into his phone, while waving for Branden to come forward in the hall. "Ricky? We've got a dead professor here. No, Newhouse. Right—protest marches at the courthouse—that guy. I'm going to operate on the assumption that he was murdered. So look, Niell, we need more people at those farms. OK, who? That's a start. I want your roadblocks up again. *Now*, Sergeant. No. OK, call in Wayne County, then. This is all going down in their backyard. I know, so listen, lock them in a barn if you have to. Both families—all of the Erbs. I don't care, just call me when it's done."

When the sheriff switched off, Branden asked, "Who's out there, Bruce? That's a lot of people to protect."

"Five minutes, Mike, and we're gonna have this covered."

Branden started off toward home and called back over his shoulder, "I'm going out. Call Ricky."

* * *

Ricky Niell's first roadblock on 229 was set up in front of the old St. Genevieve Church at Calmoutier. Branden cleared inspection with the Wayne County deputies there by displaying his reserve deputy's badge, just as Niell drove up from the other side of the barricade. Niell flipped his cruiser around in the cemetery driveway and took Branden back to the Erb farms.

There were no streetlights, and no lamps burned in either of the houses. The grocery store where Benny Erb had died was locked and dark. Niell parked on the road and led Branden down the driveway of Enos Erb's place, saying, "We took Willa Banks out of here a half hour ago. She was cursing a blue streak, but she's safe."

Branden followed. He had armed himself with a shotgun from Niell's trunk. Ricky had his pistol out. Taking careful steps in the dark, they made their way down the muddy drive to the dairy barn behind the house. Not a single light showed anywhere on the property. The only sounds were the low murmurs of dairy cows in the pasture.

At the barn, Niell pushed sideways on the tall wooden door, rolling it on its overhead casters. He squeezed through the opening, and Branden followed into the stillness.

Inside, the darkness was nearly complete. Some thin shafts of moonlight streaked down from holes in the old, high roof, but it was not enough to illuminate the interior.

In the black darkness, Niell said, "They're all in here, toward the back."

As Branden's eyes adjusted to the night, he began to pick out the straw hat of an Amish man, or the white cap of an Amish woman. Ricky snapped the switch on a micro light, and Branden saw the front edge of the group, men standing closely together in front of women and children. Ricky's light jumped briefly over their faces, and Branden saw wide, peaceful eyes watching him. There was little fear, here. What the professor saw was mostly resignation. And although some of the children's faces communicated excitement or alarm, the faces of the men and women showed passivity, conviction, and peace.

Short Enos Erb pushed forward from the group and eyed the guns with animosity. He waved at the weapons as if he wanted them to vanish from the men's hands and said, "Guns have no place here."

Branden answered, "We have to assume he'll come here, Enos."

Enos shook his head. "This is a fearful way to live, Professor."

"I know," Branden said, "but it is necessary. We find it necessary to act."

Sadly, Enos replied, "We know. We know about this, with you English, Professor. But, please, you must not kill on our account. We cannot cooperate with killing."

Niell said, "If you'll just stay here, Mr. Erb, we'll catch this guy. You aren't safe until we do."

Enos nodded with profound sorrow. "We reject the English killing."

Branden asked, "Can you just stay here a little longer, Enos? Can you stay here and let us work?"

The dwarf stepped silently back among his people.

*   *   *

By daybreak, the roadblocks had captured nothing. Branden and Niell had walked the farm roads, and that too had produced nothing. There was no sign that Eddie Hunt-Myers had been anywhere near Calmoutier. So, from the barn emerged first Enos and then Israel, followed slowly by the others.

Enos gathered his family at the back of his house, and Israel walked his family across the road. Unable to argue, Branden and Niell watched the children file back inside their houses, and soon life on the two farms resumed as if nothing in the world could harm them.

The Amish men and a few of the older boys went into the barns to milk cows and goats. Vera Erb brought out a basket of laundry to hang on the line. Israel Erb opened his store and lit the gas ceiling mantles. An older boy rode his bicycle out onto the road and turned east toward the feed store.

Branden said to Niell, "At least they're keeping the youngest children inside."

Sarcastically, Niell said, "Yeah, Mike, there's that."

37

Thursday, May 17
8:45 A.M.

THE PROFESSOR drove his truck toward home and was waved through the roadblock at St. Genevieve Church. In Mt. Hope, he stopped at Mrs. Yoder's Kitchen and got a cup of coffee to go. He drank it as he drove. In Fryburg he called the jail and learned from Ellie that Sheriff Robertson had John Hershberger in an interview room with Bishop Andy Miller. Branden asked Ellie to tell Robertson he was headed into town.

When Branden walked down the pine-paneled hallway past Robertson's office, he could hear the sheriff bellowing from Interview B, and when he entered the room, he found Robertson at the left head of the metal table, fists planted aggressively on the cold surface of the metal, chin jutting out like an angry boxer. Miller and Hershberger sat submissively at the other end of the table, eyes focused on the blank tabletop. Branden took a seat next to Miller.

Robertson took note of the professor's position next to the Amish men and pushed off his fists to stand to his full height, his barrel chest communicating dominance like a fighting cock.

Branden made a show of sighing and said in a tone of long-suffering forbearance, "Bruce, what are you doing?" From years of experience conducting interviews together, he trusted that Robertson would play along, and he wasn't disappointed.

The sheriff said in a rough tone, "Mr. Hershberger, *Professor,* admits that he lied about Benny Erb's phone."

Branden looked to Hershberger, and the preacher flicked his eyes up briefly to acknowledge the professor. Then he pointed them back at the tabletop.

Bishop Andy Miller argued, "Sheriff, the sin of this falsehood is obvious, but no one was hurt. The children are safe."

Robertson flung his arms into the air and blew out exasperation. "You had no way to know that you'd get Albert back!"

Preacher Hershberger kept his eyes lowered and said, "He promised he'd send Albert home if I gave him the phone."

"You can't be serious!" Robertson spat.

Holding up his hand to ward off further outbursts from the sheriff, Branden asked Hershberger, "How did you make the exchange?"

Hershberger looked up briefly and said, "He told me to put the phone in the back of the St. Genevieve Cemetery, behind the Haas headstone. That's what I did. Then, Albert came home."

Robertson stepped to the door and yanked it open. It was obvious that he was through talking. He glowered at the two men. "You're both being charged with interfering with a felony investigation!" he barked, and marched out of the room.

* * *

A half hour later, Branden sank into the low leather chair in front of Robertson's desk. The sheriff had a pencil out, drumming the eraser against his cherry desktop as if he were pacing the oar strokes on a slave galley—cruising speed, battle speed, ramming speed.

Branden slumped in his chair, ankles crossed, as he always did when he needed to think in the sheriff's big office. He listened to the drumbeat of the sheriff's pencil awhile and said, "He never saw him. Hershberger, I mean. Hershberger never saw the kidnapper. I can't get anything out of him to help us."

Robertson barked, "They're both going to jail!" and Branden shrugged his acquiescence.

"Mike, this is nuts," Robertson said. "If we're right about this kid Eddie, he killed Benny Erb, Cathy Billett, and maybe even

Aidan Newhouse. And he terrorized two Amish children. What kind of a college are you guys running up there?"

Bitterly, Branden answered, "We can't prove anyone was actually murdered, Sheriff."

Robertson pounded his desk with the flat of his hand and said, "He did it all, Mike. Your Eddie Hunt-Myers, *the Almighty Third,* killed three people."

"Probably," the professor admitted.

"And you think he's still here?"

"Not likely, Sheriff. Eddie's probably headed home right now. He'll probably be able to produce signed affidavits from his parents that he was home all along."

Robertson's phone rang, and he answered it, listened, and hung up. "Missy says your Professor Newhouse was a suicide. They found a note. You're probably going to be able to identify the professor's handwriting and verify that it was really suicide."

"OK, how?" Branden asked.

"Because the note is addressed to you, Mike. You two had a bad argument?"

"I wouldn't call it a *bad* argument," Branden said.

"Well, he wrote in his suicide note that you did. He wrote that you'd understand better than anyone else why he had to do it."

Branden closed his eyes and groaned.

* * *

On his way out, Branden stopped by the front counter to talk with Ellie, but she got a call, held up a finger, and answered it. As she listened to the call, Branden heard Robertson thumping down the hallway behind him. Ellie stood up beside her desk and held her phone out for the sheriff, saying, "Dan Wilsher, Bruce."

As Robertson listened, the heat and anger in his features dissipated. He let Wilsher talk and concluded with, "OK, Dan. Give it another twenty-four hours to be safe. But go ahead and take down the roadblocks now."

Switching off, Robertson said, "We're going to guard the Erbs for another day."

When he handed Ellie's phone back to her, Robertson seemed tamed by failure. The aggression was gone from his posture, and the fire was gone from his eyes.

Behind him Andy Miller said, "Sheriff, we'd like to go home."

Robertson turned slowly to the two Amish men and said, "I'm going to file charges."

Miller said, "We'll admit to what we did. You can find us at home."

Robertson eyed the bishop with more curiosity than anger and asked, "Do you know the Erbs are making it nearly impossible for us to guard them? At least that's what my chief deputy tells me."

"We live our lives, Sheriff," Miller replied. "What more can we do?"

"Right," Robertson said, as if it were a revelation to him that Amish men could be so naive.

38

Thursday, May 17
10:45 A.M.

WHEN BRANDEN got home, he found Cal Troyer's gray truck parked in the driveway and a horse and buggy parked at the curb. He pulled in beside the truck and was met at the front door by Daniel Erb. Daniel introduced himself, explaining that he had seen the professor a couple of times at his father's house.

Branden offered his hand and asked, "What can I do for you?"

Daniel said, "I understand that my Uncle Enos asked you to look into Uncle Benny's death."

"Right," Branden said. "He thought it might have been murder."

"Were you able to find out?" Daniel asked.

"Not for certain," the professor said. "It's not possible to know for certain."

Daniel thought, nodded, and said, "I suppose it doesn't matter."

Daniel took a DVD minidisk case out of his shirt pocket and handed it to Branden. The professor opened the case, took out the minidisk, and held it to the light so that he could read the label written on it: "Uncle Benny."

"Uncle Benny?" Branden asked.

"It's video, Professor. Of Uncle Benny, mostly. I thought you might like to see what he was like."

"You took the video, Daniel?"

"Yes. I like electronic gadgets. I've shot a lot of video, but the bishop says I shouldn't do that anymore. He says it's vain to make a graven image of people."

"Are you giving up videos altogether?" Branden asked.

"Yes, Professor. I've boxed up all of my disks and given them and the camera to my father. But I thought you might like to have this one of Benny. He's the only one who'd let me take his picture, anyway."

"Benny was pretty outgoing, wasn't he?" Branden said.

"He was a chatterbox, Professor," Daniel said, and smiled. He tapped the disk and said, "You'll see."

Branden put the disk back into its case and slipped the case into his pocket. He thanked Daniel, shook his hand again, and stood on the front porch to watch him guide his buggy slowly down the street. He lingered there in the morning sun, and thought of Benny Erb, Cathy Billett, and Aidan Newhouse, all dead and no way to be certain they weren't murdered. Probably they weren't murdered at all, he thought momentarily. But that was wrong, too. Someone had kidnapped two Amish children to get Benny's cell phone. Branden took out the disk and tried to imagine what he'd see when he played it. Benny Erb, he thought. Benny Erb the chatterbox.

He fished out his keys, put the front-door key in the lock, tarried a moment with his eyes closed, pushed the door open, and was struck from behind with a blow so forceful that it knocked him four feet into the house and toppled him onto his hands and knees in the hallway. When he tried to get up, he was struck in the head.

* * *

When he regained consciousness, Branden found himself sitting upright at the kitchen table, his hands taped behind his chair and his ankles taped to the chair legs. The first thing he saw distinctly was the muzzle of a silver pistol. He blinked blood out of his eyes and saw that it was a grinning Eddie Hunt-Myers who held the gun on him. With a mouth as dry as baked sand, the professor said, "Big gun, Eddie. Compensating?"

Eddie laughed and put the heavy gun on the table. He raised his hands in mock surrender and said, "You got me, Professor. I'm positively mortified."

Branden looked down at the floor and saw Cal Troyer, bound with duct tape and lying as still as death. He nodded at the pastor and said to Eddie, "You'll pay for that."

Eddie studied the professor and said, with a serene detachment, "I enjoyed that puppy, Professor."

Branden responded, "Did you kill Cathy Billett, Eddie?"

"I had to, Professor. She was in charge of Lobrelli's genetics-class genealogy chart. She knew the whole clan, inside and out. One night this week, after we had gone to sleep, I found her up reading my thesis on my computer. She knew it was a fake, but tried to hide it."

"How unfortunate for you, Eddie."

"It was! The last thing I needed right then was some snoopy girl who could turn me in."

"Did you kill Aidan Newhouse, too, Eddie?"

"There, Professor, we have an unfortunate turn of events. I'm afraid he really did kill himself."

"How did you get Benny Erb up a ladder?"

With a wide smile, Eddie said, "I didn't. I just picked him up and dropped him on his head."

"And the oatmeal?"

"Nice touch, don't you think? I climbed the ladder and poured it all over him. Fooled them all."

"Why did you have to kill him, Eddie?"

"That's on Professor Lobrelli, Dr. Branden. She's the one who's really responsible for all of this."

"Because she nominated your thesis for the Walton?"

"If she hadn't done that, I wouldn't have had to kill Benny. As it was, I had to shut him up."

"But you didn't get the phone, did you, Eddie?"

"Can't plan for everything, Professor."

"So you trashed his apartment, looking for the phone. That's why the Erbs had to clean the place up after Benny died."

"My, oh my, Professor. You're a quick study."

"Apparently not quick enough, Eddie. Why are you here? You could simply have gone home, and we'd never have made a case against you. Not one that would stick."

Eddie pulled Daniel Erb's minidisk out of his shirt pocket and held it up to the light. "Those Amish teenagers, Professor. You just never know what they'll do."

"Daniel?" Branden asked.

"Right. He's been the tricky one all along."

"What are you talking about?"

"I've been following him, Professor. You know he has a buggy with electricity?"

"So?"

"It's got lights, Professor. And a boombox wired to a car battery under the carriage. And he likes computers, this Daniel does."

"You followed him?"

"You're slowing down on me, Dr. Branden. Of course I've been following him. He's the only Amish person who stood a chance of hurting me, once I got the phone back."

"But you did get the phone back, Eddie. What could he do?"

Eddie reached into his pants pocket and brought out a cell phone. "Benny's cell phone," he said and laid it on the kitchen table. "The event log on this phone shows that somebody downloaded the call information onto a PC the day after I killed Benny. That would have to have been Daniel, Professor. He uses the computers at the library all the time."

"You think he dumped the phone records?"

Eddie nodded.

"And you think that's what's on the disk he just gave me?"

"What else, Professor? I saw him give it to you."

"It's video, Eddie!" Branden spat. "It's pictures of Benny!"

Eddie considered that and said, "Can't take the chance, Professor. Can't assume it's not those phone records."

"Go take a look at it, Eddie. The laptop's in my office. Be my guest."

Eddie laughed. "I don't know what trick you're up to, Professor, but it doesn't really matter what's on that disk at this point, does it?"

Branden stared at Eddie blankly. The irony of the situation paralyzed his thoughts. With effort, he brought his mind back to the immediate problem, and asked, "Why are you telling me all this, Eddie? You plan to kill us all, too?"

"You'll all be the victims of a home invasion. What alternative do I have?"

"For starters, Eddie, you could have written an honest thesis."

"What fun would that have been?"

"Then, you could have left little Albert and Mattie out of this, Eddie."

"Again, Professor, what fun would that be?"

"Do you realize you've traumatized two of the most innocent little kids on the planet?"

"They'll get over it."

Branden stared at Eddie and gambled on something Missy had said. "You could have said 'No' to your mother."

Eddie flared into instant and fierce aggression, vaulted out of his seat and around the table, and hoisted Branden and the chair off the floor. He carried the professor into the family room, dropped the chair angrily to the carpet, and struck Branden on the back of his head with a bunched fist.

When Branden looked up, he saw Caroline strapped to a recliner with what appeared to be an entire roll of duct tape. Caroline's head was taped, too, covering her eyes and mouth and matting her long hair. The professor groaned and said, "I'm here, Caroline. I love you."

"Oh, so touching, Professor," Eddie said. "How numbingly commonplace of you."

Branden said, "Get your gun, Eddie, and then cut her loose. She's just a woman. Let her go, Eddie. You can shoot her if she causes trouble. She can tend to that cut on your forehead. I gather the pastor gave you a fight."

Caroline tensed against her bindings and scowled furiously. Eddie laughed and stepped back into the kitchen. When he returned with his gun, he said carelessly, "Looks like your friend in there isn't going to make it, Professor. I had to club him pretty hard."

Branden tested his bindings and said, "You'll be doing yourself a favor, Eddie, if you just let us go."

Eddie's face froze. He took a folding knife out of his pants pocket, snapped the blade open, and moved toward Caroline.

Branden lunged against the tape that bound him to the chair and cried out, "Don't you touch her!"

Eddie turned back with an infantile grin and mocked, "Don't you touch her! Don't you touch her!"

Again, Branden strained his arms to stretch the tape, but it was too strong. He watched in desperation as Eddie closed on Caroline with his knife. Abject terror infused his veins as Eddie raised his knife.

Eddie held the knife against Caroline's neck, turned the sharp edge to her skin, and looked back to see Branden's reaction. Caroline pulled back from the knife as far as she could manage, but Eddie stroked the blade across her throat and drew a thin line of blood. Then he sliced at the tape binding her to the recliner, and in a single slash, he cut her free. Again he turned to Branden and laughed.

The knife went next to Caroline's ear, and again Eddie drew blood. But he simply cut the tape loose from her eyes.

Caroline pulled her hands free and peeled the tape away from her face. She started to work the tape out of her hair, but Eddie said, "Leave it, Caroline. I like it that way."

Caroline eased herself out of the recliner and took a tentative step toward her husband. Eddie stepped in front of her and held up the knife. He moved closer to caress the tape in her hair, fixing on it as if it were charming. She pulled away from him, and he laughed again. "You go make us some coffee, pretty lady," he said. "I want to be perky for all the fun."

Caroline stepped around Eddie and locked her eyes on her husband's as she passed into the kitchen. She knelt beside Cal and laid her gentle hand on his head. Then she got busy with the coffeepot.

Eddie watched her in the kitchen for a minute and then returned to the family room to sit in the recliner, facing Branden. He held the big gun out and played with it and the knife as if they were nothing more than sandbox toys. A distant focus appeared in his eyes, as his mind turned inward. When he looked up, Branden asked, "Have you had a lot of girlfriends, Eddie? Has it been fun playing one off against the other?"

Eddie focused his eyes on the professor and smiled. "More than you'd believe, Professor. I took them all up to the bell tower, too. Billett was the first to *jump*." He laughed ironically.

Branden nodded. "How did you get up there, Eddie? Have a key?"

"Since my first day here, Professor. President Laughton gave it to my daddy, so we could stand up there and see all around. Daddy gave it to me, and Laughton never asked for it back."

Stalling to give Caroline time, Branden said, "He probably forgot you had it."

"Naw, Professor. He asks about it from time to time. Says it's his responsibility to keep track of it."

"Did anyone else know you had that key, Eddie?"

"No, just Laughton."

"Since you're going to kill us, you might as well tell me what you did to those Amish kids. Albert and Mattie."

Eddie seemed suddenly arrested by an intensely visual memory. He smiled like the damned and said, "I made her rub her hands in that puppy's guts. I made him wipe blood on her face. I gutted that puppy right in front of them."

"Do you know what harm you've done them, Eddie? Do you have any idea at all?"

"Why, no, Professor. I really don't have a clue."

"I believe that, Eddie. I believe you really don't get it at all. But, do you know what the parents of those children are doing right now? They are praying for you. You sacrificed the innocence of their children on the altar of your criminal narcissism, and they *pray* for you. They pray that you will change. That you will repent."

"There is no innocence, Professor. You don't get it. The monsters are everywhere. And there is no changing. No repenting. We are what we are made to be. Nobody changes. Nobody has a choice."

"The Amish are innocent, Eddie. All of them."

"Give it time, Professor. Just give it time. Have the children been deprived? No, they're spoiled. Are their futures mortgaged to the legacy of a simpleton father? No, their futures are secure. Have their mothers crept into their young beds yet? No, but give it time, Professor. The monsters are everywhere."

Branden heard the coffeemaker growling in the kitchen, and he heard Caroline's mug cupboard open. He needed time. He needed to give her time. His mind worked for an angle, an advantage. He thought of the thesis. "How did you get your thesis past Newhouse?" he asked, desperate to distract Eddie.

Eddie came back to the present slowly. "What?"

"How did you get Newhouse to approve your thesis, Eddie?"

Eddie's mind was focused on a strange and distant realm, so Branden tried for shock. "We're going to revoke your degree, Eddie. Your thesis is a fraud."

Absently, as if it were a small matter, Eddie said, "Newhouse will accept any thesis so long as he likes the introduction."

Branden asked, "What's that about, Eddie? Cults?"

"Just trash the Christians, Professor, and Newhouse loves it. He hates 'em. He's a zealot."

"Or he was," the professor said.

"Yes, he was." Eddie seemed to be drifting on the memory of some ancient pain, rehearsing the wrongs done against him.

"Do you hate Christians, too, Eddie?"

Eddie's response came from a feral place in his mind, but his voice held no emotion. It carried no empathy. No humanity. He might have been dreaming of slaughtered puppies, or of flowers—it was all the same to him. It signified nothing. "It's your turn, now, Professor. Then your wife's."

He rose slowly from the recliner and pushed the barrel of his gun under his belt. He lifted his knife and advanced.

And stopped.

Caroline was standing in the doorway with a double-fisted grip on a black revolver, her feet planted wide.

Eddie took a quick glance at the professor and saw a grim, knowing intensity in his eyes. He looked back to Caroline while raising his pistol from his belt, and Caroline shot him three times in the chest.

39

Thursday, May 17
1:30 P.M.

THEY TOOK Eddie out in a black rubber body bag, while Caroline and the professor waited on the back porch. Pat Lance directed the forensic team collecting evidence, while Bruce Robertson stood back and let her work.

Missy Taggert came out to the porch, took one look at Caroline, and returned a moment later with her medical bag. Taking out a pair of scissors, she stood behind Caroline's wicker chair and cut the duct tape out of her hair. The professor watched in a sluggish state of shock, and the women talked softly about Caroline's ordeal.

When Robertson waved for him, Branden stepped through the family room and kitchen, down the hall to the front door, and out to the ambulance where Cal lay on a gurney. The professor climbed into the back of the ambulance and sat next to Troyer. Cal struggled past his concussion to ask, "Caroline?"

"Going to be fine, Cal," Branden said.

"Who knew she could shoot?" Cal asked.

"I counted on that," the professor said.

"When did she learn?"

"She's been training at the gun club, Cal, times being what they are."

Cal closed his eyes and drifted for several seconds. When he opened his eyes, he said, "I called Rachel Ramsayer, Mike."

Branden smiled. "That's good, Cal. That's a good move."

"No DNA tests yet," Cal said. "But I figure it doesn't matter."

* * *

When Missy had the tape out of Caroline's hair, she left Caroline with the professor and went looking for her husband. Branden sat holding Caroline's hand, hoping that she would talk. Wondering what to say. Wondering if she had been pushed too far.

"Why did he cut me loose, Michael?" she asked in time.

"He didn't see you as a threat."

"He should have."

"Caroline, he used women as playthings. Why would he credit you with courage?"

Tears started spilling out of her eyes, and the professor knelt in front of her and pulled her forward on her chair and into his arms. Softly, he said, "This is good."

* * *

After the ambulance had taken Cal to the hospital, Branden and Robertson stood outside on the cul-de-sac. Pat Lance was satisfied with the evidence she had collected. Missy Taggert was sitting with Caroline in the living room. The men had little to say to one another. They were just shaking themselves free of the adrenalin. Dumping the anxiety. Freeing themselves of Eddie Hunt-Myers.

While they stood there, Willa Banks drove up in a battered green truck coughing blue-gray smoke. She rolled her window down next to the professor and called out over the loud engine, "I heard you got him."

Branden started, "My wife . . ."

"Shot him, I know," Willa finished. "The whole town knows."

Branden found himself smiling, thinking that Willa herself probably had something to do with that.

Coarsely, Willa barked, "You know that Rat Puke Miller is gonna take Hershberger back?"

"I heard."

"Funny bunch," Willa said. "I may have underestimated them."

"Probably you have," Branden replied.

＊　＊　＊

Late that night, Arne Laughton knocked on the Brandens' door. Then he rang the bell.

In the bedroom, Branden said, "Should I get that?"

Caroline said, exhausted, "Maybe you'd better, Michael." She was finally starting to relax. Starting to think normally. Starting to hear better, after the violence the gunshots had done to her ears.

In less than a minute, the professor returned to the bedroom. "It was Arne Laughton."

"He left?"

"I never opened the door."

"What are you going to tell him, Michael?"

"Nothing, Caroline. I've got nothing to say to the president."

40

Monday, May 21
10:45 A.M.

THE BLUE-BOOK exams, which the professor had read only once, finally claimed his attention. He sat in his office and listened to Lawrence Mallory's coffeepot chatter. He had been at it for two hours, and he had written a grade, this time in pen, on the front of each exam.

From his doorway came a high, reedy voice. "Your wife said I'd find you here, Professor."

Enos Erb stood in front of the taller Mallory. Lawrence wore a bemused smile as he held two mugs of coffee.

Branden got out of his chair, came around to the front of his desk, and shook the dwarf's hand. He pulled a chair over for him, and Lawrence handed Enos a mug of coffee after the dwarf had climbed up onto the seat.

Enos said, "Thanks," to Mallory and added, "It puts a bounce in my step."

Erb sipped at his coffee and seemed reluctant to speak. The professor waited. This would be one of those long English-Amish give-and-take conversations. It'd no doubt take time. The Amish kind of time.

Eventually, Enos said, "I'm not supposed to be here."

"I know, Enos," Branden said.

"The thing is," Enos said, "we owe you thanks."

"You don't really, Enos. No thanks needed."

Enos acknowledged the irony of his situation with a fatalist's shrug of his shoulders. We live; we die. It is in God's hands.

"The thing is, Professor, I came to you for English justice."

"I know, Enos. I think you got it."

"I got all I need, Professor. I got all of that I'll *ever* need."

Branden asked, "How are the children?"

"It's slow. They're slow to mend. We take Mattie across the street to see Albert, but it's so slow. We sit them down together, and they talk to each other. They won't talk to anyone else."

"And Albert's hair?"

"Coming along."

"His eyes?"

"Sometimes, Professor, . . ." Enos choked. He cleared his throat and began to cry softly. Branden took his coffee mug from him, and Enos fished his handkerchief out of his side pocket to dry his eyes. The little man took the coffee back and finished, "Sometimes, Professor, I don't understand."

"Sometimes," Branden said, "I don't either."

* * *

After transmitting grades to Laura Pope, the professor walked toward home. He was in a Montana State T-shirt, an old pair of jeans, and leather sandals. It was a warm afternoon, with the rumble of low thunder sounding off to the west.

As Branden reached the edge of campus, Arne Laughton drove up, parked at the curb, and got out. Branden stood on the sidewalk and waited for the president to come around the front of his car. He waited for Laughton to speak.

"You've left quite a mess, here, Professor. I don't see how we'll ever get over this."

Branden remained silent.

Laughton thought he had a sympathetic ear, and he confided in Branden, "I'm going to fire Ben Capper. Letting a murder take place on our campus—what incompetence!"

Still Branden held silence. The president could well be talking about either Cathy Billett or Aidan Newhouse, and likely knew too little of the real facts in either case to form a legitimate opinion.

Laughton said, "I've got to figure out a way to talk to the Hunt-Myerses. If we can only get them to see this our way, Mike."

Slowly, Branden set his briefcase on the sidewalk and turned back to the president. "Arne," he said, "I'm at a place where I'd hand you my resignation for the simple pleasure of watching you try to replace me. But I won't. I've got a few things to do yet before I retire."

"Like what?"

"Like read the thesis of each of Nate Wells's students who's died. Cathy Billett's sophomore essay, too."

"OK, well, great. I'm still going to fire Ben Capper."

"No, you're not."

"What?"

"You're not going to fire Ben Capper."

"And why is that, Branden?"

"First, because he doesn't deserve it. At least not from the likes of you."

"Well, he's gone, so get used to it."

"Here's the thing, Arne. Are you listening? Try to keep up. I've got time to say this only once. Aidan Newhouse hadn't carefully read a single whole thesis in the last five years, maybe ten. Now, trace that out to the logical conclusion, if you can."

Laughton showed puzzlement, either at Branden's tone or at his challenge. The professor did not care which.

Branden continued, "I can prove Eddie Hunt-Myers's thesis is fraudulent. I'm going to have Laura Pope revoke his degree."

"Like that's going to matter now, Branden," Laughton said, mind ranging over a dozen distressing eventualities.

"You still don't get it, Arne. I'm going to form a committee to read every senior thesis Aidan approved in the last ten years. Nearly three dozen of them. We can revoke those degrees, too."

Now, Laughton understood. "You wouldn't!"

"You can imagine the chaos, Arne, if even half of those theses were successfully challenged."

Laughton's face wrinkled into a frown as deep as his fear. He thought about the consequences, and his face pulled tight. But as he contemplated Branden's warning, recognition of the hard reality settled into his features.

"You wouldn't," Laughton whispered.

"You sign a letter to the Board of Trustees stating that Ben Capper has your full and lasting confidence, and have a copy faxed to every professor on campus. Have it done by tomorrow morning, nine o'clock. Send the original to me."

"You can't be serious, Branden."

"If you don't do that, Arne, I suggest you take a 'long jump off a short pier,' as a student recently put it, because I swear I'll put an end to your miserable career—if you don't back off Capper."

"What makes you think you can make good on that threat, Branden?"

"I'll tell you, Mr. President, just exactly how I can do that."

Laughton stared at the professor as if he'd been speaking a lost dialect. "What? What are you talking about?"

"Your key to the bell tower, Arne. I've got it, and I'll use it to end your career if you go against Ben Capper."

"I don't believe you. I don't believe you have it."

"You need to, Arne. You need to believe me. I took it out of Eddie's pocket after Caroline shot him."

41

Wednesday, May 30
2:45 P.M.

WHEN RACHEL RAMSAYER'S plane landed at Cleveland
Hopkins Airport, Cal Troyer and the Brandens were waiting beside the baggage claim conveyors. The professor watched the
monitors to confirm when the plane had arrived, and then he took
a seat along the far wall, letting Cal and Caroline wait at the bottom of the down escalator. As he sat there, Branden took out the
folded note Aidan Newhouse had written. Reading it again, he
struggled with emotions so surreal that he wondered if he'd wake
up from some kind of weird, sadistic nightmare. But the page in
his hands was real, and he had memorized the words Newhouse
had written.

> Mike, you're the only one who will understand this. And I am
> sorry for putting this on you. It's the integrity question. That's
> it, really. I always figured I had the kind of integrity that would
> make my politics legitimate. But I don't. I've lost it somewhere.
> I surrendered it to Eddie Hunt-Myers. Most of the clowns at
> this college wouldn't understand this if you wrote it out for
> them, but I thank you for your willingness to confront me.
> Thank you for your willingness to hold me to my own stan-
> dards. I take it as a compliment. But now, I see myself all too
> clearly, and I cannot live with the person I've become. I can't
> stand to think of seeing you on campus, watching for that
> look in your eyes. That knowing look that you won't be able to

hide. I could take it from just about anyone but you. So, well, that's it, really. Tell my son I forgive him. Tell Arne Laughton to go to hell. OK. Anyway, thanks.

*　*　*

When Branden looked up from Newhouse's note, Cal was standing in front of him, a small suitcase in his hand. With a bemused smile, Cal said, "They're waiting on one more bag, Mike," and nodded toward the luggage conveyor.

Branden looked over and saw Caroline standing next to an improbably short young woman dressed in blue jeans and an Emory University sweatshirt. She was a dwarf.

Branden looked questioningly up at Cal.

Cal shrugged and said, "Her great-grandfather—my grandfather—was Amish, Mike. I suppose there's always been a chance that someone among his descendants would be short."

Branden looked back at Rachel and Caroline. Rachel turned toward him, smiled broadly, and waved.

Branden waved back, turned to Cal, and asked, "You going to be OK with this, Cal?"

A little nervously, Cal said, "She's an Ellis–van Creveld dwarf. It's the genetic syndrome some Amish descendants have. And my grandfather was a descendant of Samuel King, who came to eastern Pennsylvania in the mid-1700s. He's the start of the genetics. Samuel and his wife. Thing is, Mike, we always knew this was possible. My grandfather came to Ohio from Lancaster, and that's where the syndrome is most prevalent."

"You don't have to explain anything to me, Cal. She's your daughter, and that's all I need to know."

"I know," Cal said. "I'm a little nervous. Things have been taking me by surprise, lately. I feel like I'm always a step or two behind where I'm supposed to be, and I can't seem to catch up with my life."

Branden stood up, smiled, and said, "OK, Cal. Let's go meet your daughter."

42

Friday, June 1
8:30 A.M.

"SO, YOU'RE all packed?" Ellie asked, standing behind her counter inside the north door of the jail.

"Packed and headed out of town," Caroline answered. "We've got the top down."

"That's a long way to go in a Miata," Ellie remarked.

The professor said, "We plan to stop a lot."

Ellie said, "I'll get the sheriff," and she reached across her desk to pound on the wall, yelling, "Hey Bruce! Company!"

Robertson came through his door like a bowling ball knocking down pins. "Ellie, I told you . . ." and saw the Brandens.

The sheriff rolled up to the counter and tried to glower at Ellie, but she would have none of it. "Bruce," she sang, "you have company."

The professor tried to hold a serious expression but failed. All smiles, he asked, "Sheriff, can you send a car past our house once a day? Keep an eye on things?"

Robertson started a nod, but Missy came out of his office and handed a mug of coffee to her husband before he could finish his answer, saying, "Of course we will."

Robertson rolled his eyes and said, "How long will you be gone?"

"Don't know," Branden said. "Maybe a month, maybe the whole summer."

"We'll take the two-lane roads," Caroline said.

"The whole summer?" Robertson asked.

Branden shrugged as if there were nothing out of the ordinary about it.

"It might be prudent for them to stay out of town until fall semester," Ellie said.

Robertson asked, "Why's that?"

The professor took a brass key out of his pocket and laid it on the counter. "Because of that," he said.

Bruce and Missy waited for an answer. Ellie already knew.

Caroline said, "That's the key to the bell tower that Eddie Hunt-Myers used for four years. He got it from Arne Laughton."

The sheriff frowned and asked, "Where'd you get that key, Mike?"

"Took it out of Eddie's pocket, after Caroline shot him."

"Mike, that key belongs in my evidence locker," Robertson complained.

The professor smile and said, "I can voucher that key right now, Bruce, if you insist. But I'm willing to bet that you'll let me keep it. For a while, anyway."

Robertson remained silent and let the ire in his expression demand an answer from the professor.

Branden said, "The key, Bruce, is not material to any criminal charges that you can press."

"So," Robertson asked.

"You can't try Eddie for any crime, now."

"It's evidence, Mike," Robertson insisted.

"Right. It's evidence that can be used to best advantage in a civil suit."

The big sheriff's expression softened, as if he were saying, "I'm listening."

"Bruce, I'm going to explain the importance of that key to Cathy Billett's parents. In Montana. I'd like to give them the key, and let them consider how they might use it."

"Dang, Mike, that's cold," Robertson said.

Caroline said, "That's what I thought, at first."

Ellie said, "No, Bruce, it's not like that. Eddie had that key because Arne Laughton let him have it. That's how Eddie got Cathy Billett up to the bell tower, using that key—the one that Laughton secretly let him keep."

"Why would a college president do that?" Missy asked.

Branden shrugged and said, "Because his parents were wealthy donors."

"He let their son have a key to the bell tower because they were wealthy?" Robertson asked.

"Wealthy *donors*," Ellie corrected.

"Right," Branden said. "Wealthy donors. When I see the Billetts, I'm going to explain to them how their daughter died. I'm going to explain why Eddie had that key. I'm going to give them that key, if they want it."

"They'll sue the estate," Missy said. "For wrongful death."

"Right," Branden nodded.

The sheriff shook his head and said, "They ought to sue the college, too."

"Right," Branden said. "By the time fall classes start up, I expect we'll have a new president."